The Diva and the Beast

The Diva and the Beast

WHO WILL BE TAMED IN THE END, THE DIVA OR THE BEAST?

A WHIRLWIND ROMANCE NOVEL

D'STARR

BLACQUE STAR ENTERTAINMENT

Dazzling your mind page by page, chapter by chapter!

BLACQUE STAR ENTERTAINMENT
P.O. Box 321234
Houston, Texas 77221
© 2018 by D'Starr

Distributed by Itasca Books

Printed in the United States of America

ISBN-13: 978-0-9904966-9-4
LCCN: 2016954064

ACKNOWLEDGMENTS

I would like to thank my family and friends for believing in me and continuously being my motivation to complete this process. This is only the first book of many, and I thank you for your patience and support. Special thanks to: my grandmother, Edith J. Miller (May 9, 1931–February 14, 2015), for helping me to develop my love of reading and romance, and for guiding and supporting me in all my endeavors, I love and miss you; and my mother Cheryl R. Price (May 25, 1955–August 16, 2015), for always telling me to go after my dreams and showing me what a real gladiator is.

Prologue

CAESARS PALACE, LAS VEGAS

I spotted him immediately—tall, muscular, and dangerous. Damn! He was hot! The animal magnetism emanating from him was palpable. I walked toward the ballroom, ignoring the temptation he posed, trying to figure out how I would get Eedie into this reception. I didn't know what we were doing here, as she had been extremely secretive about the whole situation. Somehow, I knew it had something to do with the guy she met in Dallas. She was evasive, and acted weird whenever I questioned her about him. If I didn't know better, I would say she was in love.

I felt his presence before he spoke, his accent causing tingles to rush up and down my spine.

"You lost, beautiful?" he questioned.

I turned around to face him, his presence dwarfed me. He was about six-foot three, two hundred-plus pounds of deliciously handsome male. He had piercing blue eyes; a strong, aristocratic nose; squared jaw, and straight, even teeth as well as a devilishly handsome smile. He dominated the space, his shoulders were broad and muscled, the steel-gray suit he wore sculpted to his massive frame. A crisp white shirt stretched across his impressive chest and was tucked into matching gray slacks that encased powerful thighs. His tie was composed of alternating steel-gray and ice- blue diagonal stripes that accentuated the color of his eyes. His hair was cut low, almost bald, and his skin was tanned but not the artificial type; it came from spending long hours in the hot sun. His lips were a sensuous seduction; and I couldn't help wondering what they tasted like.

"Do you like what you see, *chéri*?" His voice commanded my attention, the accent causing my stomach to contract with alarmingly intense pleasure. I couldn't help blushing at being caught ogling him. He seemed to delight in my inspection, as he then took his liberty in completing his own appraisal. I swear my skin burned where his eyes assessed every inch of my body, as if he had physically caressed me. The plum-colored sheath I wore molded to every curve of my five-foot-seven frame, its strapless form allowing a languorous perusal of the exposed caramel skin of my shoulders and arms. I could feel my ample bosom tighten from the effect, my nipples straining against the confines of my demi-bra. I felt feverish and unconsciously brought my hand up to massage the ache in my chest that his evaluation evoked, moving slowly to caress the sensitive skin of my throat that longed for his kiss.

His eyes flailed me with awareness, the depths of those ice-blue orbs glistening like glaciers floating in the North Sea. I could feel my core tightening—a dull ache that became a distinct throbbing that spread warmth from within. Damn! I had never been filled with such desire. My skin tingled as if an electrical current traveled between us, and I took an involuntary step toward him before responding.

"*Oui, tout á fait!*"

His nostrils flared at my response. My French, a little rusty and colored by my Caribbean accent, brought a devious smile to his face. *God!* When he smiled, his face became less predatory and softened to an almost boyish appearance. The effect he had on me was swift and relentless. The nectar of my womb slowly escaping my body was testament to the smoldering passion between us. I slid my hand to my stomach, the desire so strong it caused the muscles there to clench almost painfully. The motion was not lost to him, and he took a step toward me, the predator once again apparent in his piercing glacial eyes, a color so translucent, they were almost clear.

What possessed me to flirt with this beast, I knew not; it wasn't even in my nature. I took a wary step back, the corner of his mouth lifting, knowingly, causing me to freeze where I stood. Somehow, I knew to show weakness to this man was to lose the battle completely. *Battle? What the hell am I thinking?* That thought ran along the lines of permanency, and I didn't even know his name. The need to flee was riding me now, but I refused to budge as he continued to scrutinize me with his captivatingly blue eyes.

A movement to my left drew my attention, and I saw Eden Rose approach, her countenance shattered. The sight of her was like cold water dousing my flaming desire, grounding me back in reality and the reason for my presence at the reception. Tears pooled in her eyes, and I ran to her, my arms wrapping around her, in an attempt to comfort her, as I tried to determine what as wrong.

"Ieshelle, I have to go!" she announced before her gaze shifted from me to the Frenchman. "You . . . you stay," she suggested.

"Of course not, Eedie!" I turned back to the Frenchman, only to see that he had been surrounded by a small army of fawning women with paper and pens in their hands, vying for his attention. *Who was he?* Our eyes met briefly before I broke the connection and squeezed Eedie comfortingly as I led her from the ballroom. "Are you okay?" I questioned her, wondering the same about myself. For some reason, the chance meeting with the beast of a Frenchman had shaken me to my core, and I was unsure of how I would fare in its wake.

One

DALLAS, TEXAS

I could feel the warm sun, on my face. The leaves of the avocado tree swayed in the breeze as the sound of my mother's voice filled the air. The air was fresh and tangy, carrying the taste and smell of the sea. I could hear Antonio, his feet soft against the grass, as he attempted to sneak up on me. We played this game often. Just when he thought to scare me, I reached up and wrestled him to the ground, tickling his ribs. His laughter filled the air.

Antonio grew quiet, his body no longer shaking with glee. I looked at his face and was shocked that I couldn't distinguish his features. They were obscured by something. I reached up to touch him only to see my hands covered in blood. Suddenly, my stomach began cramping. I looked down to see blood pooling beneath me. All I could do was stare at my hands in horror before the sound of my mother's screams filled my ears. I could feel my heartbeat quicken as the scream built within my chest, and just when it reached my lips, my eyes flew open—and the familiar furniture of my bedroom greeted me.

I was sitting up in the bed, my nightshirt clinging to my frame. My throat was raw from the screams that had escaped me during the nightmare. I took a few deep breaths. It had been a long time since the terrors of my past had plagued me. I wiped my eyes, the tears slowly falling as I remembered the pain and loss. The dream had been a combination of two terrible moments from my past—the death of my brother, Antonio, merged with the last incident with my ex, Damien, the one that resulted in the loss of our baby. My hand inched along the scar that ran along my side. It had somewhat faded with time but was still a vivid reminder.

I reached over and grabbed the phone, immediately dialing my mother's number before noting the time and then hanging up. It was three o'clock in the morning. She would be sleeping, and did I really want to bring up Antonio? She never talked about him, never reminisced, as if the pain of his loss was still too much to deal with. Besides, she had been complaining of being tired constantly, and her doctor had even suggested that she rest more. In typical Sophie fashion, she still did whatever she wanted.

I dialed the second most important person in my life, Eden Rose, my best friend. The phone rang so many times that I was about to hang up when her sleep tinted voice filled the receiver.

"Shelly? What's going on? It's three o'clock in the morning."

"Eedie, I . . . I just needed to talk."

"What's up, Sis?" she questioned, sleep no longer coloring her voice.

"Bad dreams."

"Damien?"

"Kind of. Antonio too."

"Hmmm, it's been a long time since you've had nightmares, Shelly."

"It was . . . it was so vivid, Eedie. I could . . ." I paused a second, unable to speak as pain filled my chest. Tears slid unchecked down my face yet again.

"Ieshelle, it's okay. Just breathe," Eden Rose advised.

"I . . . I still wonder every now and then, Eedie, what it would be like if they were still here, both of them."

"Shelly, you can't dwell in the past. You know this. You're young, beautiful, and successful. You still have a chance at happiness. Hell, look at me. I thought I was hopeless, that my mother and father's relationship had killed my belief in love. I never thought I would ever find someone, and now I have Jacob."

I thought about Eden Rose and Jacob and couldn't help but to smile. Their relationship began with a hot stare across a crowded room

4

that developed into a whirlwind romance that shook Eedie to her core and made her face issues from her past. She was happily married now. I couldn't deny the pang of envy that she had found her other half. It made me wonder if I would ever find the right man for me. I thought Damien had been the one, but he turned out to be a devil in disguise.

I couldn't help remembering deep blue eyes. The Frenchman. What was it about him? *I can't believe I am still thinking about him after three months.* Hell, I didn't even know his name, but I remembered the distinct attraction and the sound of his voice caressing me.

"Shelly, are you listening to me?"

Eden Rose's voice shouting into the phone brought me back. "Yeah, sorry. I was just thinking . . ."

"Hmmm, let me guess. The Frenchman?"

"Maybe . . ."

"I'm really sorry about that, Ieshelle."

"Eedie, we have already discussed this. How were you supposed to know that Jacob was dancing with his sister? You thought he had gotten married, but what you saw was a big misunderstanding?"

"It sure would have saved me a lot of time and heartbreak."

"Eedie, you know what Momma always says: everything happens for a reason."

"That's true, and Momma Jones is always right. You remember that as well. The experiences from our pasts have helped mold us into the women we are today."

"Eedie . . . what if I still don't know who I am?"

"Sure you do, Ieshelle. You're my sister and my best friend."

Yeah, but is that all I am meant to be? I thought. *I want more. I want what you have found, Eden Rose.* "Where are you?" I questioned, needing to change the subject.

"Right now, we are on our way to Virginia. The next race is at Martinsville."

"So when will I get to see you?" I asked.

"Soon. We should be in Vegas in a month. Jacob has a race at Las Vegas Motor Speedway."

"A month huh?"

"Yeah, we can go shopping, catch a show, and then go out to eat at that fabulous tapas restaurant off the Strip on Paradise."

"Sure, that's one of my faves, and I could always use some new shoes."

"That's true," Eedie agreed. "There is always room for shoe candy. How long are you going to be in Dallas anyway?"

"Maybe one more week. My office manager is still on vacation."

"Shelly, have I told you just how proud I am of you."

"Only a thousand times," I replied.

"Well, I mean it, Ieshelle. Damien really hurt you, emotionally and physically. I always thought that if I had been there . . ."

"Eedie, you yourself said I can't live in the past, so neither can you. Damien, not you is responsible for what he did to me. Besides, like you said, he helped to make me into the woman I am today." *And if I keep saying it, I will believe it*, I thought.

I looked at the clock and realized it was going on five o'clock. I wasn't going back to sleep, but that was no reason for me to keep Eedie up. I could head into the office and get an early start on the stack of paperwork that was waiting for me. Some employee evaluations were due, along with scheduling the new- hire orientations.

"Shelly, I love you."

"I love you too, Eedie. I'm better now." And I was. I would bury myself in work like I always did. "I'll call you later, okay? Tell Jacob I said hi and good luck this week on the track."

"Will do. And Shelly, you know you can call me any time. We take care of each other."

"Yeah, I know, Eedie. Talk to you later."

As I ended the call, I rolled out of bed and prepared for my day, leaving the terrors of the past behind.

Two

Albuquerque, New Mexico

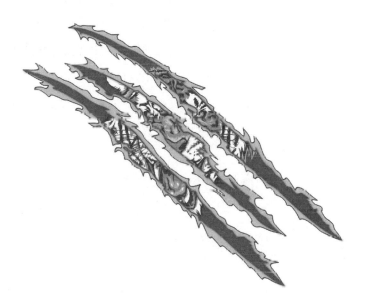

The sun was scorching hot as I rounded the corner to the gym. It was almost two in the afternoon, and I was supposed to meet Frank for a scheduled workout. My acting session had run over, and I was running late. I was practicing for a role in an upcoming action film. It was a supporting role, but it could kick off to more movies, which was my game plan. Before the acting session I finished a commercial for one of my sponsors, and now I had at least five hours to put in at the gym before I headed home. The schedule was hectic, but it would all pay off in the end.

I parked my F150, checking the parking lot to see if Frank's truck was there already. Sure enough, the black Expedition was parked in his usual spot. Frank was standing outside the door as if he was about to get in. I grabbed my bag and hopped out of the truck. "Hey what's up?" I called out.

"You're late again, Nicolas."

"Damn, Frank, shit just ran over a little."

"Yeah, well, shit has been running over a lot lately, St. Pierre."

"I know, I know. I have a lot on my plate right now."

"We all do, but you need to find your balance—and quick." Frank turned and headed into the gym. He was right; I was doing a lot, but that was what it took to get to the next level. Frank knew it too. Hell, because of our success, his gym, Zen Studios, was now one of the most sought training facilities for mixed martial arts fighters.

As I opened the glass doors of the gym, the smell of pain and sweat was familiar. I had honed my skills over the past five years in gyms like this all over the country, and world, gaining knowledge everywhere I went. Now, I had an arsenal of techniques that defeated opponent after opponent. I finally had the coveted title of Heavyweight Champion of the World. Only now, I had to put in the work to keep it.

"Okay, Nicolas, we are going to work your legs today," Frank announced.

"What's the plan?"

"Start out with Tabata on the stationary bike."

I walked over to the bike and prepared myself mentally for the workout. Tabata is a form of high-intensity interval training for cardio. I generally work out for twenty seconds and then take a ten-second rest, and repeat it for eight cycles. I had to go all out during the twenty seconds in order to get the maximum benefit. Frank stood by, his stopwatch in hand, as he monitored my progress.

"Next up, barbell complex cycle," Frank directed.

I warmed up with a set of deadlifts for twelve reps before starting my cycle of fives. The cycle included deadlifts, stiff-leg deadlifts, cleans, and front squats. I would complete each of these exercises for eight reps and then do two push-presses and then five squats. From there, I would do two good-mornings and then move on to single-leg bodyweight squats for both legs and jumping lunges until I maxed out while wearing a weight vest. I would finish up with body-weight standing calves and then rest for ninety seconds before repeating the entire workout five times.

It was a hellish routine, but it would help build my strength and endurance. Afterwards I would then rest for thirty minutes to an hour before getting in a sparring match, and then I would be finished for the day. For the next two days, we would focus on my upper body, and then I would have one day off from workouts before repeating the cycle. I knew I should probably use that day to sleep, but I would be making some appearances, shooting another commercial, and then I had the acting classes. It would be another full day.

"Nicolas, the fight is a week away," Frank pointed out.

"I know." I also knew what he meant. Any other time, I would be in Las Vegas already settled in and completely focused on the upcoming fight, but with the movie and all of the appearances and obligations for the sponsors, I felt like I was being pulled in a thousand different directions.

"Mark Hiden has it out for you, Nicolas."

"I know," I replied, but I was not in a position to say no to the sponsors. There were levels to this shit, and in order to reach the next level, I had to keep the sponsors happy, I had to keep the movie producers happy, and I had to keep my agent and manager happy. After the movie was shot, things might settle down, but as of right now, my life was total chaos. I took a deep breath, attempting to refocus my energy on the workout.

The gym was the only place lately that calmed me, but it wasn't enough. I was working hard but for what? My family, yeah. My mother and father were comfortable, now that I had achieved my title. They didn't have to worry about the mortgage, and my sister, Nicolette was well on her way to becoming a renowned chef. I was proud to have helped them achieve their dreams, but what about me? I thought I had everything—fast cars, money, women. I was living the life, but it all seemed empty to me now.

Unable to stop myself, I thought about Caesars Palace. I attended the wedding reception of one of my sister's friends. Nicolette met Alexis when she was in Europe, studying European cuisine, and they had become fast friends. The reception was taking off when I had to step outside to catch a phone call. I had just finished the call when I spotted . . . her . . . across the room. The plum-colored sheath fit her perfectly, hugging her curves and accentuating her delectable figure. She was about five-foot seven, with a caramel complexion to match her eyes. Her hair was short, in tight wavy curls that were longer at her crown and fell across her brow.

The connection between us had been instantaneous and undeniable. Never had a woman affected me so intensely. Her eyes sparkled with awareness, and I knew she felt the intensity as well. Her presence brought out the feral nature in me, and I wanted nothing more than to toss her over my shoulder and carry her away. And if my instincts were correct, that was exactly what she desired as well. Damn, I should have gone after her, but her friend's distress seemed to have closed the door of opportunity.

I took a sip of water as I started my ninety-second rest, attempting to refocus on my workout. I would be back in Las Vegas in a week. *Maybe I could find her then.* After three months, the desire she evoked had not waned. I had Nicolette question Alexis about her, but she couldn't place her by the description. I shook my head as I pushed those thoughts out of my mind and focused on the workout Frank was putting me through. Maybe I would be so tired tonight that she wouldn't plague my dreams. *One can always hope,* I thought as I restarted my routine.

Three

I leaned back in the chair, finally finished with the report I had been working on all morning. I stretched the kink in my neck as I looked over at the clock. It was going on one o'clock. *Damn, where did the time go?* My stomach started a slow growl, reminding me that I hadn't eaten since the bagel and coffee I'd consumed at six this morning. I picked up the phone receiver, intending to dial out for lunch, only to have a familiar voice chastise me in a Caribbean accent. "Ieshelle, is that you, girl?"

"Yes, Momma."

"You called me this morning and didn't leave no message, girl."

"I'm sorry. I didn't realize the time, and when I did, I didn't want to disturb you."

"What happened?"

I paused, not wanting to upset her but not wanting to lie either. "I'm okay, Momma. I called Eden Rose. We talked."

"Eedie, eh. What bothering you that you calling Eden Rose at three o'clock in the morning?"

"I had a bad dream."

"Let me guess—Damien."

"Yeah, but . . . but I'm okay."

"No, you're not. You are just going through the motions. Why haven't you started dating again, Ieshelle?"

"Momma!"

"Damien hurt you. He made you doubt yourself and your ability to judge people, men in particular. Hush now," she directed as I sniffled into the receiver. "You canna live your whole life in fear of making the same mistakes as you did then. You're not the same girl you were then. You're a woman now; ye'don changed, *girl*. You're not the same as you was then— you're better."

"Momma." My voice grew tight with emotion as the wisdom she spoke poured over me.

"Don't make the same mistakes I have, Ieshelle. Time waits for no one. Before you know it, time will have passed, and your chance at happiness will no longer exist."

"Momma, Antonio was there as well." She grew so quiet, I feared she had hung up. "Momma?"

"I'm here, Ieshelle."

"Momma . . ."

"Ieshelle, think about what I said, okay? I have to go. Sheba needs me to let her out."

"Momma . . ."

"What is it, Ieshelle?"

"I love you, Momma."

"I love you too. Remember what I said."

"I will."

I held the phone long after she had disconnected the call. *Did she feel that she had wasted her life, grieving over Antonio, or was there more to the story?* I hung up the phone and walked over to the office window that looked out over the bustling city.

Aside from my father, my mother never dated anyone other than Antonio's father, not that I knew of. Antonio's Dad was a marine she'd met while we were living in Jamaica. He had come there on leave with some of his buddies during the Sumfest, the annual reggae festival. I think she picked him because she knew he wouldn't be around, and she was lonely at the time. Antonio was born nine months later. Three months after his birth, Momma received a notice in the mail that his father had been killed in an explosion in Afghanistan.

But what if she was talking about my father? Did she regret something that happened between them? I tried to talk to her about him on several occasions, but she would always start crying, and I felt guilty for making her so sad by bringing him up. I didn't even know his name. It wasn't listed on my birth certificate. Then, after everything with Damien, I figured maybe my father had hurt her so bad, physically and emotionally, that she didn't want me subjected to his cruelty. I know I hadn't wanted my baby subjected to Damien; it was the reason I had been leaving on that fateful day.

I wiped my hands over my face, no longer hungry, and returned to my desk to start the next report, pushing everything from my mind but the numbers and figures on the pages in front of me.

Four

I was just stepping out of the Epsom salt-laced bath when my phone rang. I quickly wrapped a towel around my waist and grabbed the phone; it was my mother. I groaned silently, realizing I had failed to call her today. She probably thought something was wrong.

"Nico, are you okay? You didn't call today."

"I'm sorry, Momma. I was busy."

"Tsk-tsk. To think you would forget me. My heart is broken." I couldn't help but smile at her ability to make me feel guilty, even though she was thousands of miles away.

"*Pardonnez-moi, Momma. Toi et Papa sont jamais bien loin de mes pens*ées."

She laughed. "I know we are never far from your thoughts, but it is nice to hear so every now and then."

My heart warmed with the sound of her happiness. When I was younger, I promised myself that I would see to it that she had more to laugh about, for too many times I had witnessed her weeping secretly in despair. "How is Papa?" I asked.

"Fit as ever. He is currently tending to his animals before he settles in for tonight."

"Just where I would expect him to be." My father loved the farm it had been in our family over a century. Before I made it in MMA, it had been mortgaged to the hilt and falling apart. Now it was my father's pride and joy after I had it completely renovated, and paid the mortgage off.

"Are you okay, Nico? You sound tired."

"I'm fine, Momma. I just had a tough workout today, and then there was a commercial and the acting lessons for the movie."

"Seems like a lot."

"Yes, but if everything works out, it will be for the better."

"Nico, your father and I have told you before how much we appreciate your generosity, but I don't want you to feel obligated to provide for us."

"Momma, we have discussed this. I want to provide the security you need to be happy."

"Yes, but at what cost?"

"Momma."

"Nico, you work so hard. Make sure you do not miss out on life. Do not overtax yourself."

What she said mirrored my own thoughts from earlier that day. But if I wanted to reach the next level of success, I had to make some sacrifices. I wouldn't be able to fight forever. I wanted to set myself up so that I had a career after my time in the cage was over.

"Nico, two of the ladies in my knitting circle still have daughters who are available. When will you be home, dear? I could organize a dinner party and invite them over."

I couldn't stop the fit of coughing that erupted at the thought of meeting these women. The last time I came home, Momma had organized one of her famous dinner parties and nearly every eligible woman in the parish had turned up. "Hmmm, I'm not sure, Momma. I have the big fight coming up in a week. Will you and Papa make it?"

"You know your father, Nico. He doesn't like to fly, but I will work on him. I would love to go to Las Vegas and see one of those fancy shows."

I smiled, knowing that my mother would never change my father's mind. He had only attended fights that were scheduled where they could drive or take a train or bus. He believed if God intended men to fly, he would have given them wings. *I miss him.* "Nico, we are not getting any younger. We would like to see you settled down before we pass."

"Momma."

"Well, it's true. All of the women in my circle do nothing but go on and on about their children who are married or getting married, and they show all their grandchildren's pictures."

"Momma, have you spoken to my sister today? Maybe you should give her a call. She is the one who at least *is* in a relationship."

"Bah! That boy won't last; he can't handle her. But now that I think of it, she hasn't called today either."

"Well, you should be able to catch her if I let you ring off now," I suggested, not at all remorseful about targeting my sister for my mother's guilt trip. "Momma, I promise I will call you tomorrow."

"*Bonsoir, amour. Doux rêves.*"

"Good night, Momma." I couldn't help but laugh to think of my sister's face when my mother suggested she come home for one of her famous dinner parties.

Five

TWO WEEKS LATER

T he office was bustling as physical and occupational therapists checked in and picked up their assignments for the day. The nurses on staff were long gone, already deep within the busy traffic to make their early morning appointments. I couldn't help smiling.

The home health care agency was flourishing, with all of the staff currently booked and ads in the local paper for additional staff. I had taken a chance moving to Dallas and an even bigger risk with the second office in Las Vegas, but it was paying off. I was looking over some paperwork, a proposal to start another office in Houston. The projected net income was excellent, and business would be fluent, as the Texas Medical Center was a mecca for medical services. Besides, one of the doctors who referred patients here in Dallas had already drummed up some promising clientele for us.

I ran my hand through the medium-length bob I was now sporting—I decided to grow out my hair again. The cut was good, and the strands now brushed my shoulders. I visited my Dominican stylist for a blowout recently and was happy with the results to my naturally curly locks. The look was chic and confident, a woman on the move. I looked at the pictures that littered my desk—one of my mother, another of Eden Rose and her new husband, Jacob Preston. I smiled at them. Eedie looked beautiful, with love shining from her eyes. The familiar pang of envy stabbed my chest as I wished I had someone who adored me as Jacob loved Eedie. He worshiped her, and she him.

The Frenchman! Thoughts of him had plagued me these past months, and fathomless blue eyes colored my dreams at night. I was lost! No one compared to the wide breath of his shoulders and the animal magnetism he exuded. How could one man make such a huge impression on me? I didn't even know his name, yet I found myself comparing every man I met to him— and they all came up short. None made me burn as he did; none had the allure. Their eyes were the wrong color, their skin not toned enough, and they didn't have the right accent. *Shit!* I stood up and paced, needing to release some of the tension those thoughts had stirred.

I paused at the mirror in my office, noticing the effects of this over abundance of energy. I had lost about twenty pounds in the last three months, not that I really needed to. Previously a voluptuous size twelve; I was now a curvaceous size nine. I was blessed with long shapely legs that were currently displayed in a mid-length black pencil skirt. My stomach was tight, the beginning of a six-pack developing from the added crunches in my twice- daily workout. My breasts were still full, the double-D's sitting high, encased in the turquoise shell I was wearing, paired with a bright pink suit jacket. I accented the outfit with a lime-green belt, earrings, necklace, and bangles. The lime-green four-inch pumps I wore had intricate pink, black, and turquoise detailing. Makeup was minimal, just some eyeliner and mascara, to highlight my honey-gold eyes, and a little gloss on my lips. Altogether, the outfit was bright and eccentric, capturing my personality perfectly and would probably have looked ridiculous on anyone else but came off appearing chic and high-end. I looked good! In fact, I had never been this small in my adult life.

I walked back to the desk, plopped down in my chair, and once again looked at the picture of Jacob and Eden Rose. Longing filled my chest again. As if on cue, the intercom sounded with Tania's voice, announcing that I had an important call from Las Vegas on line one.

Only my mother could be calling from Las Vegas. If it was someone from the other office, Tania would have specified. What was so important that she was calling me at work? I looked quickly at my calendar to make sure I hadn't missed any important dates. With none noted, I picked up the phone.

"Hello?"

"Ms. Ieshelle Jones?" A strange man's voice filled my ear. *Who was this?* Some intuition signaled me, and I knew the message I was about to receive would affect my entire existence.

"Yes, this is Ieshelle Jones. How can I help you?"

"My name is Dr. Daniel Donado. I am calling from Mountain View Hospital in Las Vegas. You are listed as the next of kin for a Ms. Sophie Jones."

Next of kin? What the hell was going on? "Yes, Sophie Jones is my mother. What . . . what's happened to her?" My mouth suddenly felt like it was filled with cotton, and a huge lump lodged in my throat.

"She has suffered a ruptured brain aneurysm and is currently being prepped for surgery to stop the bleeding. I apologize for the delay in contacting you, but she was found by a neighbor, and the paramedics who responded are unsure of how long she was down. The bleeding in her brain is severe."

I couldn't breathe. I did my best to suck air into my lungs, but it wasn't working. I closed my eyes and tried again, this time taking in a small amount of air past the lump in my throat.

"Ms. Jones?" the doctor said. "Are you still there?"

I found myself nodding my head, only to realize that he couldn't see me. I must have made some sound to confirm that I was still there because he continued.

"Ms. Jones, please come as soon as possible. Does your mother have a living will or a Do Not Resuscitate order?"

Living will? DNR?

"Ms. Jones?"

"Yes, I'm still here," I whispered.

"Does your mother have any of these items?"

My mother is still so young. A living will? DNR? We have never talked about those things. "She does not have anything like that. Please, Doctor, do whatever you can to save her," I pleaded.

He proceeded to inform me, in detail, about the surgery and asked if I had any questions. I said I would be on the first flight I could arrange and left my cell number with him. I sat with the receiver in my hand for several minutes after he ended the call, numb and unsure if what I had just experienced had actually happened. I don't know how long I sat there before something within me snapped to attention, and I started making calls. I got a flight at four o'clock that afternoon—which gave me two hours to get everything together and get to the airport on time.

I called Tania into the office and informed her that I was returning to Las Vegas due to a family emergency. I wanted all immediate and urgent matters to be routed to the Las Vegas office. Anything else would have to wait until I knew more about what was going on. The office manager was still on vacation. I would have to leave Tania in charge until she returned. Moving like an automaton, I completed the rest of the work that littered my desk before grabbing my shoulder bag and heading out the door. I pulled out my cell, dialing Eden Rose's number as I slid into my rental car.

"Shelly, what's up? I thought you weren't going to call until later tonight."

"Eedie . . . " I moistened my lips trying to get them to function properly, the lump once again affecting my voice. I had to tell her what was going on. My mother had been like a second mother to her. *Had been?* Is like a second mother. *Why was I thinking in past tense?*

Eedie must have picked up on the tension I was feeling because she started shouting at me. "Shelly! What is it? What is going on?"

I poured out my heart to her, trying not to breakdown in the process. I had to be strong.

Six

LAS VEGAS, NEVADA

As I looked out the window, oblivious to the scenes below, my ice-blue eyes were reflected in the glass. My arm was still throbbing, and the brace that encased it did little to ease the discomfort. I still couldn't believe the doctor said a severe ligament tear with a definite injury to the tendon. He claimed it would be weeks before the injury would be healed enough for me to return to the ring. I was still in shock that I had been subdued by Mark Hiden with an arm bar. It rankled that I had lost the match, especially coming off the high of defeating Andre Landow. I wanted the rematch—now! The desire to wipe the floor with Hiden was a burning fire in the pit of my stomach.

Weeks! Fuck that! I had worked too hard to reach my current level to fall back now. I needed to rehab and get back in the ring, but weeks without training would put me behind schedule. Frank was discussing my options with the doctor now, and Jacque Baudoin, my manager, was on the phone talking with sponsors and reps, reassuring them that I would be back on my feet in time for the next bout and would not miss any scheduled appearances. There were also the movie producers to field. I was due to start shooting in six months. Damn! Jacque informed me this morning that he had already commandeered a deal for the rematch to take place in five months and had scheduled several minor fights before the rematch with Hiden to drum up publicity, as well as to give me a chance to prepare for my nemesis.

All in all, I had roughly four and a half months to get back up to par. Dr. Marcley came back in, trailed by Frank, and started straight in with his plan, not pussyfooting around. It was one of the things I liked about Dr. Marcley. I would need at least six weeks of physiotherapy to get back in shape for the upcoming bouts. Frank said that Dr. Marcley had already sent orders over to Helping Hands and Caring Hearts, the top home health and rehab agency in Las Vegas. The physical therapist would come to my house this afternoon to complete the assessment, and rehab would start tomorrow. A tailored plan would be developed to incorporate my mixed martial arts training, conditioning exercises, and therapeutic massage with my recovery, so that I would be in top shape for the next fight.

Dr. Marcley informed me that this agency specialized in treating high-profile clients, including some professional race- car drivers, boxers, college athletes, and more. He stated their staff was outstanding and their dynamic system for rehabbing patients gave them one of the highest ratings in the state.

I felt reassured that I would be back on top of my game in time to make the first match and subsequently, the rematch with Hiden. I nodded my acceptance of the plan and turned back to stare out the window. I tested my arm again, feeling the distinct sharp pain from my elbow to shoulder and the slight throb to my upper back and neck. Physical recovery aside, I was unsure if I would mentally recover from this injury in time for the rematch—but too much was at stake if I failed again.

Seven

The call for a new admission came just as I was about to head out for lunch. I was exhausted from the hospital visits with my mother and running the two agencies. I actually welcomed the exhaustion and the steady work as well—it gave me little time to think about *him* or to worry about my ailing mother. She made it through the surgery, but her recovery was slow, and I tried to stay optimistic, but it was difficult, knowing that the chances of a full recovery were slim to none. *If she did recover, what quality of life would she have?*

Sometimes it really sucked to know so much about health care, which led me to my current position of having to take this new-admission call, as all of my therapists were currently assigned and the new therapist wasn't due to start until Monday. *I guess I can grab some lunch on my way to the assignment,* I thought. I let Michelle, my assistant, know that I would be out for the rest of the afternoon, completing a new admission, and she could call me on my cell with any emergencies. I pulled out a change of scrubs from my bottom drawer, along with a pair of socks and sneakers, and headed to my in-suite bathroom to change for the appointment.

Dr. Marcley had called personally, so I knew he was referring a high-profile client. Apparently, he was a big-time mixed martial arts fighter who required a specialized rehab plan to incorporate into his training schedule, as well as rehab an elbow/shoulder ligament and tendon injury. MMA was an untapped clientele for us, and if this job went well, it could open up a whole new list of revenue for the agency.

The royal blue scrubs with the company logo emblazoned on the left pocket in lime green stitching were standard for the therapists. I grabbed the backpack I kept on standby just for incidents like this and headed for my car. Judging by traffic, I would have to grab a smoothie to tide me over until dinner.

◆ ◆ ◆

The Southern Highlands neighborhood was resplendent. The homes in the gated community were mostly stucco builds with either a glorious view of the golf course or the mountainous terrain. There was a twenty-five-meter lap pool on site, and the neighborhood was close to Exploration Peak Park. The area would provide an adequate training ground, with the pool and nature trails nearby. I had been informed that his home gym was in Albuquerque, New Mexico, and he would be in Las Vegas only for the six weeks it took to rehab his arm. He had an upcoming fight that he needed to train for, with several minor bouts and public appearances prior to the fight, and he would have to be out of the arm brace by then.

Always one for a challenge, I pulled up outside the house on Cottonwood Canyon Court, impressed by the size and lavishness of the estate. It was a beautiful home with great curb appeal. I parked the car in the drive and grabbed my bag as I continued to work on the best plan for this patient. I was just about to knock on the door when it swung open—and the reason for my sleepless nights stood before me.

"What the hell are you doing here?" he shouted in obvious confusion and dismay.

I was taken aback by his tone, until I noted the way he was holding his arm. He reminded me of the old story of the lion with the thorn in his paw. I couldn't help the smile that graced my lips as I responded. *"Pleased to see you too, love."* I spoke the phrase in Jamaican patois, and my amusement at the predicament was not lost in translation.

His eyes sparked once again with that animalistic fervor, and I was suddenly glad for different reasons that I had taken this case.

Eight

I couldn't believe it! The siren of my dreams stood before me, and I had just insulted her. *What the hell was wrong with me?* I noted immediately the change in her appearance— her hair was longer, and she had slimmed down some, not that she had needed it. It took me a moment to take in her navy-blue scrubs, and I registered the company logo on her left pocket as belonging to the agency that was supposed to send the physical therapist for an assessment. *No fucking way!*

"So, are we going to stand here and ogle each other all day, or are you going to invite me in?" she questioned.

I stepped back to allow her entrance, taking a breath as her perfume filled my nostrils. It was the same as before, a sweet floral scent with a hint of spice, one that had plagued me night after night for the last three months. I directed her to the living room for the consultation. She took a seat in the overstuffed black leather chair, and I sat across from her on the matching love seat, with the black lacquer and glass coffee table separating us. She was very professional, placing her bag on the table and grabbing a folder from within. She sat there for a moment, silently assessing me before she introduced herself.

"The last time we spoke"—she paused before continuing— "I don't believe I had the chance to introduce myself. My name is Ieshelle Jones."

Ieshelle . . . finally a name I could place to the bane of my sleepless nights. I introduced myself. "No, no, we didn't have the pleasure. My name is Nicolas St. Pierre."

For the next thirty minutes, she grilled me with questions about my medical history, training practices, diet, various other modalities, sleeping habits, religious beliefs, and coping strategies. Her movements were sure and confident, telling of her experience and skill.

"Okay, now that the interview portion is over, I need to take your vital signs and perform the physical exam." She stepped closer, and her scent enveloped me. I leaned into her involuntarily before I caught myself. Luckily, she was distracted with the blood pressure cuff and didn't notice. She had an effortless sexuality that drew me. Her touch was warm, clinical, and efficient, and before I knew it, she was replacing the blood pressure cuff in her bag and writing down the measurements.

"The final thing I need to do is evaluate your range of motion to the injured arm," Ieshelle stated, her voice soft and reassuring. Her hands carefully removed the brace with slow sure movements. Her touch was tentative as she tested my range, slowly running her hands over the injured muscle. The act was purely clinical in nature, but for some reason, it felt like a sensuous caress. It was hard to keep my manhood from stirring in response.

"Let me know if you have any pain or if you feel the slightest strain or pulling with the following maneuvers," she instructed.

I complied, slightly wincing as she flexed and extended my left arm. *Damn, that shit hurts!* I couldn't control the spark of anger at the memory of the fight and being caught off guard and pinned into submission with the arm bar. *I submitted to no one!* "Talk to me as I work through this," she said, "It might help."

Her request broke through the anger and frustration I was feeling, and I looked up at her profile. "What do you want to talk about?"

"Tell me what is frustrating you," she suggested.

"What makes you think I'm frustrated?" I questioned, wondering how she had picked up on my feelings so easily.

"Your muscles are tensing, and you were clenching your jaw."

I immediately relaxed those muscles, and she chuckled lightly. The sound was intriguing and made me want to hear it again. I clenched my fist but then immediately relaxed, remembering her keen observation skills. I wanted to touch her, the sensation making my fingers tingle. Thoughts of making love to this woman had plagued my dreams for the last three months, and she was standing here, with her hands moving on my body. It was unreal! I only wished they were touching me in a less clinical way, but if I had to be honest, just her touch was enough to arouse me, which was partly responsible for my frustration. I couldn't even hold her properly if I wanted.

"You're very observant," I noted.

"I have to be; it's part of my job."

"How long have you been doing this type of work?"

"I've been a physical therapist for the last four years," she informed me, not once looking my way as she continued to work with my arm.

"Only four years, and you work for one of the top agencies in the state. That is impressive."

"Thank you."

"How is your friend?" I asked, wondering what had happened to the curvaceous redhead she had been with that night—the one whose distress had interrupted our encounter.

She seemed surprised that I had remembered her friend when she responded, "She is happily married now."

"Glad to see that everything worked out for her. And what about you, Ieshelle?"

Her hands faltered a moment, and I knew that night plagued her too. What would have happened, had her friend not needed her support that night? I couldn't stop myself; I reached up to stroke her cheek. She froze. I wanted her to look at me.

"Ieshelle?"

Nine

I froze. I felt scalded. The trail his finger left was like an imprint on my skin. It was already hard to maintain a professional demeanor with my hands upon his flesh, when I wanted to stroke him in a different way. I couldn't look into those blue eyes—not now! I let out a slow breath that I had unwittingly been holding. "Mr. St. Pierre—"

"Nicolas," he whispered. "Please call me Nicolas."

"Mr. St. Pierre . . ." I started again. "I have just about finished here . . ." I informed him, my voice sounding strained and breathless to my own ears. I made to move away from him, but he caught my hand, moving quicker than I expected. His hold was firm but not painful, but there was evidence of contained strength.

"What time do you get off, Ieshelle?"

His question caused my stomach to quiver in anticipation, but my business came first, and I had to maintain professionalism in spite of the physical desire I felt for him.

I looked at him then, letting him see the desire that burned like an inferno within me. I wasn't disappointed, because the same desire burned within his ice-blue eyes. I took a step back, needing to ground myself, and his fingers slipped from my wrist as he allowed me the reprieve.

"Mr. St. Pierre, I will take all of the information back from the assessment and contact you later tonight with the rehab plan. I will also e-mail a copy to the address you provided, along with contacting your head trainer. If you don't have any questions, I will be on my way." I turned then, grabbing my bag as I prepared to leave.

He was very agile for a man who had suffered a severe injury recently, as he crossed the room to stand behind me. A tingling at the back of my neck alerted me to his presence, and his smell, fresh like a spring rain, washed over me. I could feel my stomach muscles clenching again in response, and I fought the compulsion to turn around and kiss him.

"Kiss me, Ieshelle. You know you want to," he challenged. That brought me around to face him. *How could he know? What had given me away?*

"I didn't know that your desire matched my own," he said, "Until just now." He pulled me to him, with the hand of his good arm firm against my back as his lips covered mine in a devastatingly sensual assault. As I attempted to push him away, my hands became caught between us. He dominated the kiss. His lips nipped lightly at mine before licking the sting away, only to deepen the kiss, demanding entrance into the deep recesses of my mouth.

God, it had been a long time since I had been kissed like this—kissed as if life depended on the sustenance my mouth could give. I was drifting on wave after wave of passion, slowly drowning in my desire to have this man.

"Nicolas?"

The sharp questioning tone broke the spell I was under, and I came rapidly back to the surface, like a diver who had the bends. My stomach contracted in disgust as I looked over his shoulder to see a stunning blonde with long legs and an ample bosom, dressed in denim shorts and a tank top.

I stepped away from Nicolas and headed for the door at a clipped run. I could hear him calling me, and if it hadn't been for Blondie calling for his attention again, he would have caught me at the car. I sped out of the neighborhood and headed back to the office.

Ten

I can't believe this shit! I slammed the door
to the house, nearly taking it off its hinges.
Nicolette looked at me like I had lost my
mind. Maybe I had. She'd been right here,
and I'd let her get away! Damn! I kicked over
the side table, and the large red vase hit the
floor, shattering into a thousand pieces. I felt
like yelling. *Why the hell had she bolted out*

of here? I turned back to Nicolette, suddenly comprehending. She thought Nicolette was my woman. On top of everything, the first chance I got, I started groping her. "I'm going out." I announced as I headed out the door.

"Yeah, well, who is going to clean up this mess, mister?" Nicolette yelled as the door closed.

I headed out of the subdivision, taking one of the many trails that led to Exploration Peak Park. I would have gone to the gym and hit the bag if wasn't for my fucking arm. Damn, I felt like shit was spinning out of control. The loss of my title was unexpected, but who ever expects to lose? And the injury! It couldn't have happened at a worse time. I was on the verge of crossing over to the next level of success. I was so close, I could taste it, and it could all be snatched away.

I picked up the pace, starting a slow jog. Thoughts of Ieshelle Jones filled my head once again. Ieshelle—a beautiful name for a beautiful woman. I placed her accent as Jamaican or from the Caribbean islands. She was a physical therapist. I hadn't lied when I said I was impressed. I'd barely graduated from high school, spending most of my time in the gym, working out and training. Nicolette, I always teased her, had "stolen" all of the brain cells in our family, graduating at the top of our class and gaining a full scholarship to college.

I made a complete ass of myself at this first meeting. Ieshelle was a professional; she would feel I'd crossed the line by kissing her and most likely wouldn't return unless she thought I would remain professional too. I could do that, as long as I got what I wanted in the end, which was her. I had to get her out of my system. Maybe then I could focus on everything else in my life. Honey-gold eyes and caramel skin had plagued me for too long. I licked my lips, her taste still lingering there. I knew she was not unaffected by my touch. She had kissed me back, her own passion as uncontrollable as my own.

I paused as I reached the peak of the hill and looked out at the remarkable view. I would have to change my tactics. She'd run from me today. Somehow, I would have to get her to come to me. Once I had sated this desire I had for her, maybe I would finally be free.

Eleven

A colorful bouquet of tropical flowers decorated my desk while their exotic perfume filled my office. I smiled as I read the card again. It was a genuine apology, and I considered changing my mind about sending Melanie over today to work with Mr. St. Pierre, but then, I thought better of it. Nicolas was dangerous to my psyche. Never had I abandoned my professionalism in light of desire. *Besides,* I thought, *if he is involved with someone, it's better to stop this before it starts.*

Michelle buzzed in, disturbing my pondering. "Ms. Jones, you have a call on line one. It's Mr. St. Pierre."

I smiled again, hoping that he hadn't yet figured out that I owned the company. "Tell him I'm not in the office," I instructed Michelle. "Say that I'm out seeing patients and won't be in until later this evening."

Moments later, Michelle reported, "I did as you instructed. He didn't seem real happy about it."

"What did he say?" I asked.

"Nothing that I could understand. He erupted into a dialogue of French, if I'm not mistaken."

"Great. If he calls back, tell him the same thing."

I picked up one of the reports I was working on. I still had to get the Dallas office straightened out—I'd come back two weeks early due to my mother's condition. Which reminded me, I needed to call the hospital to check on my mother. She had remained stable in spite of the severity of the aneurysm. I was comforted with that, but I knew there was still a long way to go before she would be able to come home.

My mother's dog, Sheba, wasn't faring well in her absence. I had to have her admitted because she wasn't eating or drinking. It was as if she was mourning my mother already. The vet had given her IV fluids and started her on a new diet, and that seemed to be working. The vet said she would most likely be ready to come home within the next week. In spite of Sheba's ambivalent attitude toward me, I wanted her to get better.

I decided to call the hospital to speak to my mother's nurse. I looked at the report I had been working on while the elevator music played in my ear as I waited for the nurse to pick up. In spite of the success of my businesses, I would give anything to get rid of all of the paperwork. I had just finished the last page in the report when the phone clicked and the nurse picked up.

"Ms. Jones?"

"Yes, how is she doing today, Julia?"

"There has been no change."

I tried not to get disappointed at the news, but it was disheartening that her condition had not improved.

"Ms. Jones, take it for the blessing it is. She hasn't gotten any better, but she also hasn't gotten any worse. Your mother is stable. The doctors were able to stop the bleed. Now she just needs time. She tires easily but wakes up in spells, due to the constant bustle of the ICU. Once the doctors feel she is well enough to move to the floor, she will be able to rest more soundly. She will also build her strength, now that she has the feeding tube."

"I know. It's just . . . so hard to see her this way."

"I know it can be difficult to see your mother in her current condition. You are used to her vibrant personality. I have to be honest with you, Ms. Jones—she may never be the same person she once was, but she is a fighter. Do not give up on her. She hasn't given up."

"I know, you are right, Julia. Thank you for the update. I'll be by to see her at the usual time this evening."

"No problem. See you then."

I ended the call, knowing that the nurse was right. My mother was a fighter. I couldn't give up on her. Our last conversation had plagued me for weeks. *What had my mother meant about not making the same mistakes as she had made? Was I letting my chance at happiness pass me by?* I reached up to grasp one of the flowers of the bouquet between my fingers. The fragrance enveloped me once again. Nicolas St. Pierre. Fate would see fit to toss us together yet again under unreasonable circumstances. He was my client. *He was also sexy as hell!* And he was taken.

I pulled the flower from the vase, running the petals against my lips as I sat back in my chair. His lips had been firm against mine, completely dominating the kiss. He was swift, in spite of his injury. His arms had felt reassuring, wrapped around me. I felt safe. Maybe that's why I had run from him. Well that, and the fact that he had a half-dressed female already. How could he kiss me right there when she was in the next room?

In spite of the anger I felt at the fact that he did not care if his girlfriend caught him with another woman, I couldn't stop thinking about him. Nicolas continued to plague my dreams at night. I couldn't seem to stop imagining him making love to me as he whispered sweet French terms of affection in my ear.

The sound of the buzzer brought me back to the present, and I tossed the flower down on my desk, admonishing myself for my wistfulness. I picked up the phone, taking the call from one of the doctors in Houston with whom Dr. Marcley had asked me to speak regarding the new facility. I had to stay focused. My business was my life now. I didn't have room for anything else.

Twelve

It was over a week since I'd last laid eyes on Ieshelle. I continued to call her every day and knew it was no coincidence that she was always out with clients. She was avoiding me. What was I to make of that? Either she wanted nothing to do with me, or she was afraid to be alone with me. I was going with the latter. It certainly hadn't taken us long during that first encounter at Caesars Palace to determine there was an intense attraction between us. It also hadn't taken her long to stamp that desire out when she'd seen her friend's distress.

She must have jumped to the conclusion that Nicolette and I were a couple, although if I had been in her position, I probably would have concluded the same thing. I had yet to dispel that notion, as I wanted her to ask me about my relationship to Nicolette. Seven whole days passed, and she hadn't budged in her resolve to avoid me. Maybe I needed to do some research regarding her and change my next move. What I was doing currently wasn't working. I only had five weeks before I had to return to New Mexico. I had to have her out of my system before then if I wanted any chance of maintaining my sanity. Nicolette had already left for California but would be back in a few days. She was tired of my stomping around like a lion with a thorn in his paw.

I had to admit I had been at my worst lately, snapping at Frank and Jacque for every little thing. I could only identify the intense feelings consuming me as desire and lust. Once I had Ieshelle in my bed, the pressure would ebb like the aftermath of a volcano, and peace would once again return to my life. I could then focus on the upcoming fights and the movie. But what could I do to speed things along? I couldn't complain about her staff— they were truly remarkable and skilled in their craft.

I'd spent the past week with Melanie, one of the trainers who specialized in aquatic conditioning. She explained to me that aquatic exercises were low impact and would take the pressure off my bones, joints, and muscles. Water offered natural resistance that would help strengthen my muscles. When she first suggested it, I thought she was talking about swimming, but she put me through a series of exercises that I would have called arm curls, only I used aquatic hand webs and didn't raise my arms higher than the water. As my arm healed, Melanie informed me that I would eventually progress to underwater weights. Each session was followed by a deep-tissue massage.

I would bet money that Ieshelle had sent Melanie intentionally. She was a voluptuous, blue-eyed blonde who was well aware of her good looks but who still maintained a professional distance. If she was a test, I passed with flying colors. Four months ago, I would have been all over Melanie, breaking down her walls until I had her in my bed. But now, only one woman could satisfy my desire, and she had golden eyes and ebony hair. How could I get her to come to me? I contemplated that question as I prepared to make an appearance for one of the sponsors. I was running out of time. Round one went to Ieshelle. Now it was time for round two.

Thirteen

I was looking over the last of the reports from the Dallas office when Michelle buzzed in that there was a call on the phone from Frank Zen. Why would Nicolas's trainer call, unless there was a change in his schedule? I directed Michelle to put him through, the interruption a needed break from the tedious paperwork.

"Ieshelle Jones speaking. How can I help you, Mr. Zen?"

A distinct voice responded, one that had plagued my thoughts seemingly forever. "Why don't you want to see me?" Nicolas questioned, his voice caressing me through the phone.

"Mr. St. Pierre, I was informed that Frank Zen was on the line. If I had known—"

"If you had known it was me, *mon ange*, you would not have been so willing to take the call. Why is that? Why won't you come to see me? You must be in high demand, as whenever I call, you are always with a *client*."

"Just what are you insinuating?" I asked.

"Only that your skills must be superb because you are in such high demand. Am I not worthy of your talents?"

"Mr. St. Pierre, if you are displeased with any of the trainers that you have had thus far, please let me know, and I will be sure to report it to the manager."

"Now, why would I want to speak to the manager when I can speak to the boss, herself?"

I paused in shock; he knew. Well, I guess it was only a matter of time before he discovered that I had lied. *Why did the fact I'd deceived him leave a sour taste in my mouth?* It had seemed like such a good idea at the time, cover for the fact that I was the boss, leaving me seemingly inaccessible. "What do you want from me, Mr. St. Pierre?"

"I think you know the answer to that, Ieshelle, only you continue to dissuade yourself."

"Mr. St. Pierre, I'm sure your. . . friend wouldn't like my seeing you," I stated, attempting to remind him of his girlfriend . . . lover . . . whoever she was.

"She would not mind. In fact, she was quite upset that you left when you did," Nicolas stated.

His response puzzled me. "I don't know how to take that."

"Ask me, Ieshelle, and I will tell you anything you want to know. There will be no secrets between us," he replied smoothly, his voice causing goose bumps to break out over my arms.

I held the phone away from my ear, unsure if I'd heard him correctly. I took a deep breath before continuing. My heart beat in undeniable excitement at the prospect his words suggested. I asked the question that had burdened me since I had stormed out of his house. "Who is the woman?" I tried to keep my distress at the thought of him lying with another woman from coloring my tone, but I found it quite difficult. I surprised myself by the unfamiliar emotion, and I knew that this man was more dangerous than I had initially perceived the present conversation evidence of that. It was out of character for me.

"Her name is Nicolette."

Nicolette. It suited her. *What was she to him, though?* "What else do you want to know, *mon chéri?*"

How did he do that? It was as if he could read my mind. Was I ready to hear of his debauchery? Unable to stop myself, and knowing this conversation was already well outside of the realm of professionalism, I asked, "Who is she to you?" As soon as the question was asked, I wished I could retract it. It gave too much away.

"Nicolette is my twin sister, *mon ange*, you have nothing to worry about from her. She was calling me to the phone because my parents were calling from St. Isadore."

"Nicolas, I'm sorry."

"Ah, *mon amour*, if I knew that was all I had to do to get you to use my name, I would have told you about Nicolette sooner."

Realizing my folly, I took in a deep breath, knowing that I somehow had to take control of the conversation again and get it back on a professional standing. He was a client; it would not look good if the boss behaved in a manner that the staff was prohibited from displaying. It wasn't good business, and I always put business first. I need this contract to go well if I wanted any chance of opening the new agency office in Houston and then possibly another in San Antonio.

"Mr. St. Pierre, I must apologize for my lapse in behavior. I assure you that Melanie is an extraordinary physical therapist and has been briefed on your specialized plan. She should be there now to assist with your rehab exercises and to help you incorporate such into your training program. The plan we have designed is one that you can continue once the injury has resolved, so as to prevent future injury or relapse. If this session is not up to your standards, please contact the office, and I will have a replacement sent out immediately."

"Ieshelle, don't regress. You were doing so well," he taunted.

"I don't know what you mean," I said.

"Yes, you do, but I see my flattery and phone conversation skills will not be enough to get you to change your mind. Have dinner with me, *mon ange*."

How could he make the offer sound like a threat and a compliment at the same time? My heart was pounding in my chest, as images of us rolling around in a huge bed invaded my mind. Never had a man tied me up in knots as effortlessly as he had. And we had shared only one stimulating conversation and one ravishing kiss. I had to end this call quickly, before I made yet another mistake with him.

"Mr. St. Pierre, as I mentioned, if Melanie is not to your liking after your session, I will accommodate you."

"Have it your way, Ieshelle, but let me tell you one thing before you run away from me yet again. I want you, and I always get want I want."

With that said, he hung up the phone. I sat there with the dial tone sounding in my ear, loud and grating, but unable to snap out of the shock of Nicolas's admitting that he wanted me. If only I was ballsy enough to admit to myself that I wanted him just as much.

◆ ◆ ◆

The week was long, and Friday seemed like it never would come. Nicolas St. Pierre was being a royal pain in my backside. He had rejected every physical therapist I sent to work with him. He always completed the training, but at the end of the day, he found some error and demanded a replacement. On top of that, he continued to send me flowers and various other treats daily, as a reminder of his intentions. He was relentless, and frankly, I was at my wit's end. There was no way I was going back to his house. If I was honest with myself, I was scared of what I would find between us. Lust transforms into desire . . . and desire morphs into love. Love was an emotion I thought I knew and had experienced—it was overrated and pretentious, because when the passion ebbed, the love was soon to follow. Then came pain, hurt, and rejection. I shook my head, dispelling those unwanted feelings, and focused on the job at hand.

In addition to the problem with Nicolas, my mother's health was not improving, although it was not deteriorating either. The doctor said we had to look at the positive in that. She had regained some function in her right hand and leg, but she would need extensive occupational and physical therapy. Her blood pressure was still uncontrolled, and her blood sugar was elevating. All in all, I did my best to keep my head above water. I prayed every morning, visited my mother every evening, and prayed yet again at night. My mother was all the family I had.

I looked at the picture on my desk of Eden Rose. I did have Eedie, my best friend and sister, but she had a new husband and soon, probably, a new baby. That pang of envy returned to my chest, and longing filled my heart. If I was honest with myself, I would admit that I was afraid of Nicolas St. Pierre. I was afraid of going through the motions of developing a relationship, establishing trust—falling in love. But with all the wooing on his part and the relentless dreams he caused, it was probably too late. I was already halfway there.

The ringing phone was a welcome break from the monotony of paperwork, and I answered, as Michelle was out to lunch. Hearing Consetta Robinson, my manager at the Dallas office, on the phone was a shock, especially as she was supposed to be returning from her trip to Dominica. I tried to get her to slow down. I could barely understand what she was saying, she was speaking so fast. By the end of the conversation, I was concerned and quite vexed when I realized I had yet another dilemma on my hands. Consetta's husband had broken his leg in a water skiing accident and would not be able to fly until the end of the week. Once home, she would need additional time to help him until home health could be set up through her insurance company. She requested additional days off to accomplish this but was concerned because she had two new physical therapists starting, as we were losing two of our regulars— April was due to go on maternity leave, and Jessica was moving to New Mexico. There were also three new nurses starting this week, as well as a host of other things that Consetta had put off until she returned from her trip. I had completed most of the immediate issues since having to return to Las Vegas, but now it sounded like I would have to make a trip to Dallas.

I quickly started making plans for the trip, jotting notes on a legal pad. I would need to stay late today in order to fly out tomorrow and prepare everything for Monday's orientation. I decided that since I was taking the trip to Dallas, I might as well do the annual review while I was there. Once I had set my flight plans and made transportation arrangements, I pulled out the paperwork I would need for the annual review and headed to the hospital to visit my mother. By the time I made it home, it was after nine o'clock, and I had to fly out at seven in the morning. I took a quick shower and fell into bed.

Fourteen

I tried to calm myself, but my blood was boiling. I had just finished my training for the day. It had been a shock to discover that Ieshelle Jones was actually the owner and operator of Helping Hands and Caring Hearts. At least it was a complete contrast from the seductively exotic femme fatale that I'd met at the reception and the cool, competent physical therapist who visited me for the initial assessment—two very different facets of a very intriguing woman . . . a woman who continued to plague my thoughts day and night. She seemed too young to have two successful agencies in operation, as I suspected she was in her late twenties.

The amount of anger I felt initially at finding that she had left the city shocked me. *How had I become so emotionally involved with her from one kiss?* From that first conversation at the reception, she had consumed my thoughts. *Was she an obsession?* Maybe.

I threw the towel I was holding into the hamper and walked toward the shower. I had to get her out of my system! I needed to focus on my upcoming fights and the movie. *Shit!* I banged the wall, leaving a small dent in the plaster, before stripping down and dousing myself under the warm spray of the shower. I lingered in the shower, contemplating my options as the warm spray cascaded over my head.

◆ ◆ ◆

I called the office, threatening to pull the contract with the agency if I wasn't given Ieshelle's contact information to the hotel where she was staying. Michelle refused to give me her cell number. As I rang the hotel, I imagined that Michelle was probably calling Ieshelle to warn her. It wouldn't matter. I needed to get over her and quick. I had already lost round two, and I refused to lose the next round.

Ieshelle sounded out of breath as she answered. *Had I interrupted something?* I suddenly envisioned her entangled with another man, and I forgot the plan to be calm and cool.

"What the hell do you mean by sending these *blokes* over?" I demanded, not giving her a chance to say hello.

She grew quiet, and I knew she recognized my voice. "I'm not sure what you are talking about," Ieshelle replied innocently.

"A distinct possibility," I declared. "*Mon ange,* you know exactly what I am talking about. Or is it that you only appear to be an angel, but in fact you are *mon mégère,* no?"

"Maybe I am both," she declared. I liked the fact that she continued to flirt with danger, in spite of her decision to stay clear of me.

"*Mon ange*, did I catch you at a bad time?" I asked, needing to know what she was doing. She sighed into the phone, as if a balloon had been deflated.

"How did you get this number?"

"I have my ways. You sound tired. Have the last couple of days been that rough?"

"I've been busy with the agency."

"I've missed you, Ieshelle. Have you missed me?" I asked. I wanted her to know just how much she had affected me, and I was curious to know if I had affected her as intensely. I could hear her catch her breath, as if she was shocked by my admission. She grew quiet then, and I decided that she had missed me just as much. "Ah, I see you have. That's good. That means I was on your mind just as you were on mine. Did you dream about me?"

"What do you want, Nicolas?"

"You already know what I want, *chéri*, but if you wish, I shall make it plain and simple yet again. I want you."

I could hear her moving around in the room. She sounded as if she was pacing, as her breath was coming in short pants. "It's okay, Ieshelle. I am willing to admit it for the both of us."

"Nicolas—"

"Ieshelle, I wanted to tell you what I have done so that I—and I alone—will suffer your wrath. I have informed my trainers that I want my contract pulled if you will not serve as my physical therapist."

"You what? You son of a b—"

"Now, now, *chéri*. You can call me all the names you want when you return at the end of the week."

"The end of the week? But I have—"

"You have until the end of the week to settle everything you need to settle in Dallas and return to Las Vegas, or I will pull my contract. Either way, I will have what I want. Only you won't get everything you want. Think it over, *mon ange*."

I ended the call, reclining in the lounger where I was sitting, unable to stop the smile that spread across my lips. *And round three goes to me!*

Fifteen

I sat on the bed in the hotel room staring at the receiver in disbelief. I couldn't believe his nerve...and yet, I could. He didn't give in to convention; he did what he wanted and to hell with the consequences. *Shit! I can't take an ultimatum from him! I stood up, pacing the length of the room again. How the hell had he gotten this number?* I pulled out my cell phone, intending to call the office and I noticed several missed calls from Michelle's number. *Damn, I forgot to take it off silent mode.* She obviously had given him the hotel number to try to stall him, hoping she would catch me on my cell. *Damn!* He must have threatened her with pulling the contract if she didn't give him the number. She knew how much I needed the contract if I was to establish the new agency in Houston, and now there were even prospects for a new agency in San Antonio.

He was right, I couldn't afford for him to pull his contract. It would look bad with our other big clients if he pulled out.

Besides, I needed the revenue that the MMA fighters could bring if we were successful in his rehabilitation. *How dare he give me a week! And to think he still believes he has a chance with me! I was just starting to soften toward him,* I thought, remembering how relaxed I had become at the sound of his voice.

I didn't understand how he did it. It seemed like he was able to detect what I was thinking or how I was feeling. Over the last two days I had been busy with the new employee orientations, and I had just started the annual review. I needed to meet with the contractors for the new office in Houston and had a flight scheduled for later this week. I had intended to stay over and meet with the doctors from the clinic to whom Dr. Marcley had introduced me and discuss contracts and clients.

In spite of his arrogant and overbearing manner, he was right. I had missed him. I missed the daily flowers and treats that were sent to the office. And in spite of my vow to avoid him, I had asked each of the therapists for a daily report of his progress. He was right about something else. I wanted him, and in spite of my better judgment, I would have to meet his demands and return in one week. I needed his contract; there was too much at stake if I called his hand, and pulled out.

I would return in one week. I would even be his therapist, but that was it. I vowed right then that I would not give in to his charms, and I willed myself not to dream about him anymore.

Trouble was, I did dream of him that night, instead of cursing him. Nicolas covered me, and our bodies melded to- gether as he pushed deep within my core, over and over again. I woke up just before five, unable to return to sleep, glacial blue eyes haunting me.

Sixteen

It seemed to take forever for Monday to arrive. I almost thought she wouldn't show, but she arrived in a lime-green scrub set with the company logo in navy blue on the left pocket and her bag in tow, promptly at eight in the morning. I knew it was wrong of me to use the contract against her, but I couldn't contain the pleasure I had received from having her somewhat at my mercy. The feeling was quite exhilarating—I was sure she was a woman who normally took charge of situations. I decided it was difficult for her to be dominated, yet secretly she yearned for exactly that. I had resigned myself to the truth yesterday—that I was more than obsessed with her. There was something about her that called to me. In fact, I was probably halfway in love with her. How it happened was no wonder, but what did that mean?

I anticipated her anger at my manipulation, so to soften her up, I sent flowers to her hotel room every day after our phone call. I knew once she was back in Las Vegas, she would be more secure, and her defenses would be stronger than ever. I had already used the typical tactics—flowers, candy, and cards— but somehow I knew that if I truly wanted to have her, I had to do more than just possess her. I wanted to know everything about her, but I wanted Ieshelle to share herself with me willingly. To do that, I would have to overcome her wrath. Good thing I loved challenges.

Frank was standing off to the side, looking over my stats, I had just finished a five-mile run, followed by a hot shower, and it was time for my massage and arm conditioning before I did some ring training. It had been over a month since the injury, and I was progressing well with the rehab treatment. I lay down on the massage table that had been set up in the study, which had now been designated as the rehab room, as it contained a newly furnished rehab table and other conditioning equipment.

I could hardly contain my excitement at having Ieshelle with me. I only wished we were alone, but I would take what I could get.

"Frank has informed me of the workout scheduled for today," she said. "If you're ready, I will start with the deep-tissue massage before the conditioning exercises." Her voice was calm, but she did little to hide her irritation with me. I watched her as she moved with effortless grace.

"Be gentle with me, Ieshelle. I'm hurting today." *In more ways than one*, I thought, shifting to adjust for the sudden swell in my groin area. I felt like a kid in a candy store—the anticipation of being with her again, of having her touch me—even in a clinical setting—was so great that it had me hard with desire.

"Where exactly are you feeling the most discomfort?" she asked before running her hands over my arm, the peppermint oil soothing the muscle and tissue. I indicated the area that was most tender, secretly imagining her hands upon another tender part of my anatomy. Ieshelle kneaded and massaged until the muscle in my arm no longer ached, and the tissue became soft and pliant. Her hands were surprisingly strong for a woman so slight in form.

In spite of her clinical touch, it was difficult for me not to respond sexually. She smelled of citrus and spice, a heady combination. Her hair was swept back from her face in soft waves and curls, held by a thin navy-colored headband. She looked younger than before and wore no makeup today, other than a blush-pink lip gloss. Ieshelle was a complex woman, and the desire to know every facet of her only intensified during the session. I was second-thinking my ability to withstand her ministrations when she ended the session, saying she was finished. I wasn't ready for it to end, but Frank had left during the session and was now waiting in the ring out back, and I still had to put in some ring training to maintain my speed and agility.

Frank would let me complete only one three-minute round. He didn't want to overtax my arm. Today would be my first day back in the ring. I could tell just by my workouts that I was nowhere near the level I needed to be in order to take on Mark Hiden. The injury was truly a setback I didn't need. After I left Las Vegas, I would have only two months, roughly, to get back up to fighting strength before the first preliminary bout. In the midst of training, I would still have appearances for the sponsors and some obligations for the movie producers. I'd already talked with Jacque and told him to reduce both to a minimum and to schedule anything that he could now.

I finished putting on my T-shirt as I watched Ieshelle pack her things. She had just returned from the bathroom where she washed her hands to remove the fragrant oil, which she used instead of liniment. I suddenly had an idea and hoped she wouldn't get too riled up at the prospect. She looked up from her bag just as I was about to make the suggestion.

"Do you need something else?" Ieshelle asked.

"Yes, I actually do, Ieshelle. Today will be my first day back in the ring, and I wondered if you would come out back with me, in case I have any problems."

She appeared shocked, as her eyes grew wide at the suggestion, and I knew she had not been unaffected by the session. My smile of pleasure only caused her to become even more unsettled, and she took an unsteady step backward. "I really don't think—"

"It was my understanding that I was your only client, currently."

She smiled tightly, and I could tell she was gritting her teeth. "That may be true Mr. St. Pierre, I do however, have other obligations."

So, we were back to "Mr. St. Pierre" again. No problem. I do love a challenge. "I thought you might want to see firsthand some of the techniques used in the ring," I said with a shrug. "That way you could judge if I was pushing too far too soon. But if you feel my arm is okay . . ."

I could see her mind working as she contemplated what I said. There really wasn't a choice. If she didn't observe the sparring match and I was reinjured, she would blame herself for not staying. If she planned to take on more

MMA clients, it would be good business to learn more about the sport. "Where is the ring?" she questioned.

"A temporary ring is set up out back. If you have any paperwork to complete, you can bring your laptop. There is an outlet on the patio."

She balled her fist at her sides, her eyes burning me with their intensity. I could only imagine she was probably envisioning ripping my head off. I tried not to smile at her obvious dilemma. She grabbed her bag and raised her hand, suggesting that I lead the way. I wasn't too sure I wanted her at my back in her current state, but I was finding it hard to contain my amusement, so it was best she couldn't see my face. This bout went to me as well.

Seventeen

I tried to still the emotions welling inside me. I had been so angry with him this morning, and on the drive over, I thought about everything I wanted to say to him. All of that, immediately fled my mind at the sight of his half-covered body. He was fresh from the shower, wearing only a pair of basketball shorts that rode low on his hips. I hadn't noticed his tattoos before, but they were on full display today.

There was a tribal that stretched across his shoulders and curved around his upper deltoids. His right bicep had a large cross with the Canadian flag draped across it, while some vertical Chinese symbols were on his right pec. The tattoo on his left pec extended down his side and was the most intricate—it gave the impression of a beast—a tiger—tearing through his skin to get out. The detail was magnificent; the tiger's eyes were the same piercing blue as Nicolas's. It was as if Nicolas's body acted as a cage for the tiger.

His body was in top shape, in spite of his injury. His chest and abs were sculpted perfection, and his back just as defined. He was the epitome of sexiness and that along with his dominating personality made for a deadly combination.

When my hand inadvertently began to massage the muscles of his neck and chest—not the area targeted for massage—I called a halt to the session. He seemed unaware of my slip in professionalism, and I handed him his T-shirt before heading to the bathroom to wash my hands. I was taken aback when I returned to the room and saw him leaning against the wall adjacent to the bathroom, as if he were waiting on me.

"Did you need something else?" I asked, inflecting irritation in my tone to cover the breathlessness I suddenly felt at the sight of him so near. I noted that Frank had defected, and I felt like Nicolas was invading my space. I took a step back to lengthen the distance between us.

"Yes, I actually do, Ieshelle. Today will be my first day back in the ring, and I wondered if you would come out back with me in case I had any problems."

I was barely able to get through a massage-therapy session without molesting you, and you are asking me to spend more time with you? I needed the time apart to simply . . . breathe and prepare for the second session.

"I really—"

"It was my understanding that I was your only client, currently."

I couldn't hide the flood of anger I felt at his manipulation. I gritted my teeth as I reminded myself how much I needed this job. "That may be true Mr. St. Pierre, I do however, have other obligations." I was thinking of the stack of paperwork I'd brought with me to complete in between sessions.

"I thought you might want to see firsthand some of the techniques used in the ring. That way you could judge if I was pushing too far too soon. But if you feel my arm is okay . . ."

Shit! He was right. It would be in his best interest if I observed the sparring match. Besides, if I planned to take on more MMA clients, it wouldn't hurt to observe a training practice. I looked into his fathomless eyes, which sparkled with a devious glint, and I realized he knew exactly what he was doing. He had no qualms about using his contract to get what he wanted; otherwise, I wouldn't even be here. He was calculating, and my stomach contracted as I realized that I just might be in over my head.

"Where is the ring?" I asked.

"A temporary ring is set up outback. If you have any paperwork to complete, you can bring your laptop. There is an outlet on the patio."

I grabbed my bag and gestured for him to lead the way. I noted the vast open spaces within the house as we passed through the living room and headed through a set of glass French doors that led out to a covered patio. A sitting area contained black wicker furniture accented with white cushions and red throw pillows, a black glass pedestal table, and a black ceiling fan. The fan was a welcome addition to combat the warm desert climate and it moved in a lazy circle overhead. The boxing ring was to the rear of the yard, past the pool. It was set up on what appeared to be a basketball blacktop. Several guys were already working in the ring, and Nicolas headed that way after directing me where to sit.

I positioned myself so that I could watch him in the ring and work on my laptop. I still had a few annual reviews to complete and the notes for the massage therapy session from this morning to enter. I couldn't help looking up when I noticed him step into the ring. He was a warrior; his body was built to give punishment, but in spite of his size, he was remarkably light on his feet. He moved with animal grace and had his opponent pinned to the floor and submitting within three minutes. I had never watched MMA fights before taking this assignment and did not realize how brutal they could be. This was just a sparring match, but they went all out! I had to prevent myself from stopping the fight a couple of times when I noticed the extension of Nicolas's injured arm. But he always recovered and showed no sign of favoring the arm, so I began to relax.

It wasn't until he was exiting the ring that I dropped my head back to my computer screen, only to realize I hadn't accomplished one thing during the time I had been sitting there. As he stepped up to the table, I packed up the laptop, preparing myself mentally for the conditioning exercises so that I could complete my rehab session for the day.

"Get much done?" he questioned. I searched his face, wondering if he knew I had been completely captivated by watching him. He gave no hint as to whether that was the case, but somehow, I couldn't tell him the truth.

"Yes, I did." The paltry lie left a bitter taste in my mouth.

He smiled at me then, as if somehow, he could read my mind. "Come on, so you can finish up with my arm, and then we can have lunch."

"Lunch?" I squeaked in alarm. "What are you talking about?" My stomach rumbled at the thought of food—I only had a light breakfast, so I was hungry, but his comment caught me off guard.

"Yes, lunch. Nicolette prepared it for us. It's her way of apologizing for the other day."

"Apologizing?" I said in dismay. "She has nothing to apologize for."

"She feels she does, seeing as how she interrupted our. . . interlude," he replied silkily.

"Nicolas, what did you tell her?"

"I love it when you say my name, Ieshelle," he whispered.

Damn! I hadn't meant to do that; it gave him an edge, and for me to show weakness would be to lose . . . *but to lose what?* I was too afraid to examine those feelings, knowing the battle might already be lost. "Mr. St. Pierre," I corrected myself, "If you are ready, I will complete the conditioning exercises and leave you to your lunch."

"Leave?" said a soft, musical voice from the French doors leading into the house. "But you did ask her, Nicolas?" Nicolette was dressed in a short baby-doll sundress of a royal blue with white hibiscus flowers. The color brightened her eyes and accentuated her golden tresses. Her smile was friendly and welcoming, and I found it hard to refuse her sincere offer.

"I guess it will be okay to stay for lunch," I responded.

She smiled with delight and returned to the kitchen after stating that lunch should be ready by the time I'd finished with Nicolas's exercises. I walked back to the rehab room, resolving to complete the session as quickly as possible.

"Don't be irritated with her," Nicolas said, "She means well. She has been starved for female company, I'm afraid, after being cooped up here with me and the guys since the injury."

I rounded on him in anger, hoping to deflect some of the desire that reared up at the thought of touching him again. "I'm not irritated with your sister. She has done nothing wrong."

"So, you are still angry with me? I will just have to do something to change that." Before I knew his intention, he had pulled me to him, and I was pinned between him and the nearest wall. He smelled of sweat and earth and brought wanton thoughts to mind as his obvious arousal pressed firmly against my stomach. Not satisfied with the position, he bent low, lifting me until his cock nestled firmly against my core. The contact caused me to lose focus for a moment, as I leaned my head back in abandon, my hands resting on his shoulders.

Somehow in the interim, he had removed his shirt, and my hands came into contact with his warm, sweat-slickened skin. He leaned in, his lips grazing the side of my neck just below my ear, tracing the small butterfly tattoo there. The caress shot through me like a current, flooding my blood with desire like a thick bolt of lightning to settle as a slow throb in my core. I couldn't help grinding my hips against him as my hands caressed his neck. His hand drifted beneath my scrub top to brush my stomach before cupping the fullness of my breast. My nipple swelled beneath his warm touch, straining against the confines of my bra, while he placed soft, seeking kisses along my jaw. I needed his lips; I needed to taste him again. I slid my hands up to cup his jaw, bringing his lips into contact with mine.

He immediately dominated the kiss, claiming control as his lips devoured mine. I was set adrift on a sea of emotion and desire so strong that I thought I would lose my way. Nicolas, as if he could read my thoughts, kept me grounded, his hand wringing such exquisite pleasure from me. His touch caused tears to slide unchecked down my cheeks. It had been a long time since I allowed a man to kiss me . . . to touch me so intimately. That thought was like being doused with ice, bringing me up short, and I pulled back from Nicolas, breaking the kiss.

"Nicolas, please . . ." I begged, unable to voice my fear further, but, somehow he understood my distress. I was reassured of his astuteness when he began to kiss the tears from my cheeks, murmuring soft words in French that I couldn't quite catch but that still soothed my frayed emotions. He held me to him, smoothing my clothing into place, allowing me the time I needed to regain myself. My fear was vanquished by his gentleness. He kissed me one last time, not the passionate assault of before but a promise a promise of more—before he placed me back on solid ground.

"Come, Ieshelle, see to my arm so that we may have lunch," he instructed as he sat in a nearby chair. His change of subject was welcome and allowed me to pull my frayed nerves together so that I could complete the session.

Nicolas was quiet and made no mention of the kiss, not even during the delicious lunch his sister had prepared. Nicolette, it turned out, was a very talented and renowned cook. The lunch was a sample of her culinary expertise. I learned that she was to open a restaurant in California in the near future and was trying some new recipes. We hit it off well, businesswoman to businesswoman. We must have talked for ages, and I finally noticed that Nicolas was no longer participating but was idly watching me interact with his sister. Brought up short by the contented look in his eye, I insisted that I had to get back to the office.

Nicolas walked me to my car. "You are a puzzle, *chéri,* one that I choose to solve," he declared before pulling me into his arms and placing a chaste kiss against my forehead. The kiss left me wanting, and as if he knew, he stated, "Until later." Then he turned and walked back to the house.

Eighteen

I walked back into the house, unable to hide my pleasure. Ieshelle wanted me just as much as I wanted her, if her response to the kiss was any indication. The passion, I expected, but the tears...the tears were unsettling. They called to my sense of chivalry and honor. Never before had a woman reacted so intensely to my touch, my kiss. I ran my finger across my lips; her taste lingered. Just when I suspected I had figured her out, she threw me for another loop. I ran my hand over my head, unsure of what to do.

I still wanted her—there was no denying that—but seeing her with Nicolette today . . . It was refreshing to see Ieshelle smile and laugh. She didn't do it enough. The sound was infectious, and I wanted to be the one to cause her such happiness. She was visibly relaxed with Nicolette, someone she saw as her equal—both successful businesswomen. They both had drive and tenacity that would help them to accomplish all that they set for themselves. Ieshelle would have the new agency in Houston and probably many more after that, and Nicolette would have her new restaurant.

What would I have in the end? I stepped into the kitchen to see that Nicolette had already cleared the dishes from the table and was standing at the sink. I took up a familiar position next to her, lending my assistance in loading the dishwasher. Nicolette was uncharacteristically quiet, a sure sign of her displeasure. She didn't know the entire story about Ieshelle, but I could suspect what she was thinking.

"What are you doing, Nico?"

"Nicolette."

"I know you are up to something, and I don't like it. I like her."

"I saw how well you two got along."

"So, what are you doing?"

"I don't know. I thought I knew what I wanted, but now . . ."

"Don't start something with her if you are not willing to see it through, Nico."

"What are you talking about, Nicolette?"

"She's attracted to you, but for her, that's not enough."

"How did you get all that out of one lunch date?"

"How did you miss it? Ieshelle is not like all the other women you have dated, Nico. She doesn't want your money; she doesn't need it. She's not trying to use you to get media attention, and in spite of the attraction between you, she isn't falling at your feet. She's different." She slammed the dishwasher closed and stormed off to the back of the house.

Maybe I hadn't missed it at all. Maybe I had been attempting to ignore what I knew to be true. From that first encounter outside the reception, I knew attraction wouldn't be enough. I remembered the electricity that had flowed between us, but in spite of that, she had shut the switch off at the first sign of distress from her friend.

I walked outside toward the pool, grabbing a bottle of water on the way. I still had lower body exercises to complete before I showered and met the acting coach. I had only two and a half weeks before I was scheduled to leave Vegas. I thought I would be spending the remainder of that time with Ieshelle warming my bed, but now . . .

What happened to her? I felt her fear at the realization of what she had done. She had let me in. I guess I could be delighted with the fact that I had been able to get her to drop her defenses, if only for a minute. *What was she protecting? Why was she afraid to let me get too close? What was I going to do now?* I could release her from her obligation to me, but I found her fascinating. I wanted to learn more about her. More than anything, I wanted to see her smile and hear her laugh again.

The sound of Frank's voice interrupted my thoughts. "Don't get distracted, Nico. You have enough on your plate without adding a woman."

I hopped on the stationary bike and asked, "What are you talking about, Frank?"

"Don't bullshit me, Nico. Why was she here?"

"Because I wanted her to be. So?"

"Maybe I'm too late, and you are already too far gone." Frank walked back toward the ring, shouting to the two fighters in the center.

I slipped in my earphones, and the sound of one of my favorite rapper's voice filled my ears as I contemplated my next step with Ieshelle. Shit was getting complicated real fast! I needed to decide what to do about her—or was Frank right, and it was already too late?

Nineteen

FIVE DAYS LATER

F ive days since he held me in his arms—
and nothing. It was hard to accept that
I was actually disappointed that Nicolas
hadn't tried anything else since the second
kiss. The very next day he had apologized and
then maintained an irritatingly impersonal

attitude. His therapy sessions were coming along well, and his range of motion in his arm was steadily increasing. He pushed himself like no other athlete I had worked with, but I didn't understand him. One minute he was declaring how much he wanted me; the next, he was keeping me at arms distance.

I grabbed my bag from the backseat of my car and headed to Nicolas's door, preparing for yet another strenuous day, only to halt in my tracks as Frank Zen, Nicolas's head trainer, came out. He explained that he had a meeting and would return later that evening. Nicolas was currently working with his strength trainer, Jamie McGregor. I walked into the house, expecting Nicolette to be in the kitchen, cooking, as she so often was, but she was missing in action, and there was no indication that she had been there, as the kitchen was spotless. I had become fond of her, and we often talked while I waited for Nicolas to finish his training sessions. The house seemed extremely quiet, so I headed out back to see if he was in the ring.

No one was there. I wondered if I had misheard Frank. Maybe Nicolas was actually out with one of his other trainers. But if so, why was the front door unlocked? I stepped back into the house and stopped suddenly as Nicolas stood before me, a towel slung around his neck and navy-blue basketball shorts riding low on his narrow hips. He grasped the towel on each end as he slowly took in my presence. Damn, he was hot! I couldn't help tracking a rivulet of sweat at the dip in his collarbone as it descended down the hard plane of his chest. He hadn't been shirtless since the last day that we kissed. Images of him pinning me up against the wall flashed before me at that moment. I looked up to see him grinning devilishly. I couldn't help blushing at the fact that I had been caught ogling him yet again.

"Come on, love," he said, "before I pin you against the nearest wall and lose my resolve."

So, he had been thinking about the kiss too. *But what did he mean by losing his resolve? Did that mean he still wanted me?* I followed him into the rehab room and prepared for the massage therapy and conditioning exercises. We went through the established routine until Nicolas broke the silence.

"Ieshelle . . . I want to ask you for a favor, but I'm not sure if you will accept."

I studied him through narrowed eyes.

"What is it?"

"I have an appearance tonight at a benefit for Mothers Against Domestic Violence. Nicolette was supposed to accompany me, but her boyfriend flew in last night, and she is now going with him. I would be honored, Ieshelle, if you would join me tonight." I looked into his face, wondering if he knew that I was supposed to attend the ball anyway. He gave no hint that he knew about DIVAS, the women's group I formed after I left Damien. *'Distinguished Intelligent Visionaries Achieving Success'* had been my way of recovering from the pain and loss that Damien had caused. I must have hesitated too long, because he continued. "I know it's rather short notice, but I would really appreciate it."

I took a deep breath before taking the plunge. "It just so happens that I will be attending the benefit anyway, so I don't see why we couldn't go together." After the words left my mouth, I panicked at the thought of being on a date with Nicolas. *Well, I guess it isn't really a date,* I thought. *We're just going to the same event together.*

"Thank you," he said. "I will pick you up at six. Where do you live?"

I scrawled my address on a sticky note from my bag. I held the note for a moment longer than usual before handing it to him, realizing that even though this was not a date, I was letting him in. I had never let anyone come to my home besides Eden Rose and my mother. I had not been willing to trust anyone new since I left Damien. *What made Nicolas so special?*

"You can take off early today," he said. "Grant Howard is here for my boxing training, and I won't be working with my injured arm too much, so we should be finished for today."

"Okay, then, I will see you tonight at six."

"Yes."

As we exited the rehab room, a tall, athletically built gentleman dressed in sweats was waiting outside. He introduced himself as Grant Howard. I let myself out and decided that I would head to the hospital to see my mother then finish up my paperwork at the office. If I could finish there around two, I would have time to hit the nail shop before I had to get ready for tonight. Somehow, I felt like tonight was special in spite of its not being an official date. Argh! I needed to call Eedie! *What the hell was I doing?*

Twenty

What the hell had I been thinking, asking Ieshelle out tonight? *Hell, I hadn't been thinking at all.* It had been five days. Five long days and five even longer nights since I last held her in my arms. Hell, keeping up the client/ therapist relationship was taking its toll. According to Frank and Jacque, my temperament was even worse than it had been. I couldn't help it. I felt like I was wrung too tight. Every time she touched me, all I wanted to do was throw her down, climb on top of her, and plunge my sex deep within the walls of her womanhood until both of our desires were fulfilled.

The fact that she clearly still desired me only made things worse. I had resolved to wait until our professional relationship had concluded. I knew where she was now, and I would not lose track of her, in spite of my need to return to New Mexico soon. The weeks sped by and only two remained before I was scheduled to return home for intense training for the upcoming bouts. And I needed it. Frank was right by reminding me that I needed to focus. Mark Hiden had kicked my ass once; he would not get the satisfaction of doing it again.

But where did that leave me and Ieshelle? The stats on successful long-distance relationships were low, but it wasn't impossible. *I can't believe I am even thinking about this.* Three weeks ago, all I wanted to do was slake my lust, and now, I am contemplating a long-distance relationship. *What had changed?* A lot. I actually understood her now. She explained that she and her mother had lived in Las Vegas since she opened her second agency. They had moved to the states from Jamaica before moving to Dallas, where she went to school and obtained her physical therapy degree.

Somehow, I felt there was more to that story, but I didn't want to push. I relished the fact that she trusted me enough to share those small details of her life. *Damn, I have it bad!* I still continued to dream of her, but more and more, the dreams were shifting, as they no longer were filled with constant images of us pressed together in erotic play. They were replaced with visions of her smiling or laughing at something she found amusing. That was one of my pleasures—getting her to laugh. It seemed that she was almost shocked at the initial occurrences between us, as if she was out of practice. Each subsequent time I got her to laugh had been a small victory for me.

I headed back toward the ring, needing to get the time in with Grant before I had to get ready for tonight. I was actually anxious about the date. I was contemplating what I should wear when my cell phone rang. I looked at the display and groaned; it was my mother.

"Nico?"

"Hello, Momma."

"Nicolette tells me you are terrorizing everyone down there. What's going on?"

"I'm fine, Momma."

"Hmph. No, you're not. Any time you get riled like this it means something is bothering you. Is it the upcoming fight?"

"No, not exactly," I answered truthfully, knowing that if I was going to convince Ieshelle to give us a chance, I would be in for the fight of my life.

"Is it your arm, then?"

"No, Momma, my arm is healing well. Dr. Marcley said I might only need a couple additional weeks of therapy before I return to New Mexico and start my intense training."

"Hmmm, that means it's a girl."

"Wh-wh-what?" I stammered.

"Yep, a girl. I told Nicolette. You acted the same way when you were younger and caught wind of Victoria Delacroix."

"Momma, are you serious?"

My father's voice bellowed in the background. "Anna, leave the boy alone."

"You're outside with Papa?"

"Actually, we are headed into town. He's taking me to the local pub for dinner."

"What's the occasion?" I asked, wondering if I had missed her birthday or anniversary.

"We are meeting the Girards for dinner. They are here visiting their daughter."

"Oh, well, tell them hi for me. I will call you tomorrow, Momma."

"You have no time to talk to your momma?"

Suddenly, my father's booming voice filled the earpiece. "Are you good, lad?"

"Yeah, Papa, I'm okay."

"Well, don't let one good ass-kicking keep you down. It's what you do after ye get knocked down that makes a difference."

He was right—but would my desire to have Ieshelle stand in the way? "I understand Papa."

"Okay then. Don't forget to call your *maman* tomorrow. You know how she gets."

"I will. Have a good time."

He started laughing, the sound familiar and comforting. In spite of all the trials we faced when I was younger, our house was always filled with laughter. Would I have the same for myself someday? I thought of Ieshelle and wondered if she was what I had been waiting for.

Twenty-One

Six o'clock came sooner than I expected. I was just finishing my makeup when the doorbell rang. I checked my appearance in the mirror before answering the door. I'd kept my makeup light, using a menagerie of browns and golds to accent my eyes and a coral lipstick with clear gloss. My hair, naturally curly again, was swept to one side by a Padparadscha sapphire-colored stone and turquoise-embellished comb. My coral evening gown complemented my caramel complexion. The gown was trumpet-style with a matching sapphire-and-turquoise beaded waistband, ruched tulle overlay, and an asymmetrical illusion neckline. I accented the dress with turquoise, sapphire, and gold chandelier earrings and added a matching tiered bracelet of the same gemstones to complete the look. I stepped into the four-inch turquoise peep sandals with coral, gold, and turquoise crystal embellishments along the heel and toe. The embellishments at the heel reminded me of a peacock's tail. I couldn't calm my nerves and thought of girls getting ready for the prom before I grabbed my matching handbag, and headed downstairs.

The doorbell rang a second time just as I reached the first floor. I opened the door and stepped back in shock at Nicolas's transformation. He was dressed in his black-and-whites, the designer tux tailored to fit his perfect physique. He was sexuality personified, and I felt my stomach clench with the knowledge that I would be his for the night. He had removed his arm brace, and I wondered how his arm would fare for the evening.

As if reading my mind, he piped up, "It's doing okay, Ieshelle. I promise I will let you know if I have any discomfort."

I smiled, unable to fathom how he could read me so easily.

"You're gorgeous, *mon ange*," Nicolas said as he grasped my hand and brought it slowly to his lips. His eyes never left mine. My hand burned where his lips brushed my skin, the fire spreading through my veins pooling in my groin. He looked at me, that devilish smile gracing his lips—the one I was growing so fond of—before grasping my other hand. "Are you ready?"

I looked to where our hands were clasped together, a contrast in color with his bronzed fingers and my brown- sugar-toned digits. I found myself imagining how his hand would feel, running over my body, caressing me with his fiery touch. I nodded my head, signaling that I was ready, and we headed out the door. I took a moment to appreciate the sleek lines of his black Audi R8. I liked speed, and it seemed that Nicolas did too. He held the door open for me before sliding into the driver's seat. Nicolas moved with animalistic grace, and my eyes tracked his every move—I was unable to look away. I clutched my handbag, my heart hammering in my chest as desire took my breath away.

"Relax, Ieshelle," he whispered softly.

I exhaled the breath I had unwittingly been holding as his hand snaked out to capture mine again. Oddly enough, my anxiety decreased, and I started to relax.

We rode in silence until, finally, he asked, "How long have you been supporting Mothers Against Domestic Violence?"

I paused for a second before responding. "For the past four years, since I started my women's group, DIVAS."

"Who are divas?"

"It's an acronym—D-I-V-A-S—which stands for Determined Intelligent Visionaries Achieving Success. It's a support group designed to help women pursue their goals and dreams. We meet once a month for open discussion and hold workshops for various interests. Each mentee is paired with a mentor to provide a source of support, a fountain of knowledge, and sometimes just someone to listen. Once the women achieve their goal or goals, they attend a 'coronation ceremony,' or coming out, and after that, they are assigned a mentee. That way, they give back all the knowledge that they gained to assist the next woman. Mothers Against Domestic Violence is just one of the many organizations that we support."

"Remarkable. You are a remarkable woman, Ieshelle. Where do you find the time and energy for all of this? A successful business, an admirable women's support group—what else are you hiding behind those mysterious caramel-colored eyes?"

What does he mean? Has someone told him about Damien? I looked over to him again, but he was relaxed and gave no hint of prior knowledge about the most disastrous relationship in my past. I responded, hoping he hadn't caught my alarm at the question. "Every year we have a bike rally and choose a different start and finish. Last year we started in Houston and ended in Dallas."

"So, you ride a motorcycle? It suits your wild and adventurous nature," he said as he turned into the drive of the hotel where the benefit was being held. Not surprising, there were several photographers present to snap shots of the attendees, as a large number of high-profile state and local government officials would be present, as well as some celebrities. The attendant opened the door and assisted me out of the car. Nicolas came around to take my arm and escort me into the building.

The photographers seemed to go wild as we entered, snapping picture after picture, and reporters even tried to ask him questions about his last fight, his injury, and his upcoming matches. He stopped to answer some of the questions, dodging the one about his injury and the upcoming matches. I would have escaped to leave him to his paparazzi, but he held me closer to him, one hand sliding to the middle of my back while he took my other hand and held it over his heart. I knew he was an MMA fighter, but I didn't realize how popular the sport was or that he would garner such media attention. I guess I should have known, as Las Vegas was big on professional fights, and MMA was the new money-maker.

"Are you okay?" he asked, once we finally made it into the foyer of the hotel.

"Yes, I'm fine," I said, not entirely sure if that statement was true. *Was it like this all the time for him?*

Reading my mind yet again, he said, "It is not always like this, Ieshelle. They are just looking for anything now, especially since I lost my last match." The bitterness at the memory of the defeat was not lost on me. I squeezed his hand in reassurance as we entered the ballroom and were shown to our seats. The dinner would start shortly, followed by music and dancing. This event was a great place to network, and DIVAS was a big supporter. I waved to several women from the group, as well as to several officials I knew. I was pleased to note that Nicolette and her boyfriend were seated at the table with us.

After an enjoyable dinner the music picked up tempo, and people drifted to the floor to dance. Nicolas escorted me to the dance floor, where I discovered that he was a very adept dancer.

It was easy to relax with him, and I resolved to enjoy the night and whatever it might bring. It wasn't until I said that I needed a breather that Nicolas and I left the dance floor. I went to the powder room, while he headed for the bar. Little did I know that trouble in paradise would come in the form of Damien Brooks.

Twenty-Two

I walked over to the bar as Ieshelle went to the ladies room to freshen up. I couldn't keep my eyes off her. The exquisite evening gown accentuated all of her curves, as had the plum- colored sheath she had worn at our first encounter. Her shoes were equally elegant and added height to her slender frame so that we complemented each other perfectly. I ordered a cognac neat and a glass of champagne. I enjoyed attending this event—it raised money for a remarkable cause.

The dance floor was filled with dignitaries, city officials, and high-powered business people from all factions. Ieshelle fit right in, where I was on guard, expecting someone to single me out as an outsider. I took a sip of the drink, wondering why all of my old insecurities were resurfacing. I acknowledged a fellow fighter across the ballroom and noticed Nicolette heading my way.

She was shocked to see me with Ieshelle, I knew, but she remained sociable during the dinner. I knew I would hear about it later. Nicolette and Ieshelle had developed a friendship during the past week, and her warning had not fallen on deaf ears. On the contrary, it made me contemplate my intentions toward Ieshelle. I still wanted her, sexually. There was no denying the attraction that simmered between us, but the lust and desire that I'd felt initially had somehow morphed into something more. What that was, I was afraid to name.

"I thought you had changed you mind about pursuing her, Nicolas." No preliminaries for Nicolette.

I handed her the glass of champagne, and ordered another for Ieshelle as I feigned ignorance. "What are you talking about?"

"You know very well what I am talking about."

"Nicolette, you ditched me remember. Ieshelle was willing to attend the event with me only because she was already coming."

"Hmmm."

"Nicolette, don't worry. I won't hurt her."

"She might not be the only one I am worried about."

I looked at her then, surprised that she felt concern for me. "Why would you say that?"

"She's vulnerable and so are you, even if you do a better job of hiding it."

"Nicolette . . ."

"I'm right, and you know it. Just be careful."

"I will," I replied, placing a kiss on her cheek. "What about you? I thought you and Willie boy had called it quits."

"Don't start, Nicolas. I am giving him a second chance."

"Now, it seems, it's my turn to give you some advice, little sister."

"Nicolas, he apologized for what he said."

"Doesn't matter. Momma is right. He can't handle you. You're too much for him, and his own insecurities are what cause him to act the way he does—like a chauvinistic pig."

"Really."

"Really. You need someone who complements you, who you view as your equal."

"How do you know I don't see William that way?"

"Nicolette, it's me you're talking to."

"Yeah well, he's better than my last boyfriend. Gregory only wanted to date me to get close to you. Talk about man crush."

"Nicolette, don't sell yourself short. The right person is out there for you. You just have to be patient."

"Well, patience isn't something I am known for. Neither are you."

"Yes, that may have been true, but I am learning," I replied, thinking of Ieshelle yet again. I checked the time. I wanted to dance with her again before the event ended. It might be the last time I would get to hold her that close for a while.

"Go ahead," Nicolette urged. "She was probably stopped by one of her friends from the women's group. She knows quite a few people at this function."

"You're probably right," I replied, looking expectantly toward the hallway where Ieshelle had disappeared. I crossed the ballroom, unable to dismiss Nicolette's warning. *Was I vulnerable?* Maybe, but Nicolette was right: so was Ieshelle. I ran my hand over my head in frustration. *Just what the hell did this mean?*

Twenty-Three

I dashed back into the restroom after spotting Damien in the hallway, wanting to avoid the confrontation. What was *he* doing here? *At a domestic violence event, of all things?*

I started pacing, trying to think what I could do, how I could escape—but then I thought about Nicolas. I couldn't just leave him. Damn! I played at retouching my makeup and counted to one-hundred before exiting the bathroom, hoping that Damien had taken off. I was disappointed, however, as he was standing there, waiting for me, with the arrogant look I had grown to hate on his face.

"Hello, Ieshelle."

The sound of his voice grated on my nerves, but not wanting to make a scene, I smiled politely and returned the welcome before attempting to bypass him to head into the ballroom. He stepped in front of me, blocking my way.

"What do you want, Damien?" I was unable to hide my annoyance and hoped that it covered the fear that was shooting through me. *How could he stand there, acting as if he had no care in the world, when he had hurt me so badly?* I started shaking my head and demanded, "Let me pass."

"Now, that is no way to start our reunion," Damien whispered as he took a step closer. "I couldn't believe my eyes when I saw you walk into the ballroom tonight. Five long years, Ieshelle. I thought that I was over you and had stopped looking for you, but seeing you again only brought it all back for me," Damien crooned. "I know you feel it too, baby." He grabbed me to him, but I put my hands in between us to push him away. His grip was strong on my arm.

Panic choked me as I remembered another night on which his grip had gone from firm to brutal. My words were but a whisper. "Damien, please let me go."

He maneuvered me farther back into the alcove, and I pushed harder against him. The hallway, bustling with people just moments ago, was now deserted. I did not want to be alone with him. I felt like I was suffocating.

He ignored my distress. "Ieshelle, I just want to talk to you, to tell you how sorry I am and how much I miss and need you. I still love you, baby."

His words sparked my anger. "Sorry? *Sorry?* Are you sorry about cheating on me? Or, are you sorry about hitting me the first time? Or is it the second time when you busted my lip that you're sorry about? Or maybe it was the last and final time when you pushed me through a glass window, and I lost our baby!" I shouted. "Save your sorries, Damien. I don't need them, and I don't need you! I'm not the insecure eighteen-year- old you found in Jamaica and brought here with fairy-tale dreams. That girl is gone! Now let me go!" Feeling renewed strength, I shoved him away from me. His arm slipped and suddenly, I was free. I made to pass him yet again, but he recaptured me easily, spinning me around to face him. I had seen that look before, the one filled with contempt and anger, the one that would cross his face just before he struck me. I stood there, bracing for the impact, but it never came. I opened my eyes in surprise to see Nicolas tussling with Damien on the floor. Nicolas had Damien flat on his back in seconds, and his hand was crushing Damien's throat.

"Don't ever touch her again! Do you hear me? If I catch you near her, I won't be as *nice!*"

If you consider a busted lip, bruised throat, and swollen eye nice, I thought.

With that said, Nicolas turned around to gather me to him before ushering me through the ballroom and out of the hotel. I could feel the tension coming off him in waves, and I felt I needed to say something to calm him down.

"Nicolas . . ."

"Shhh! Are you okay?" he said before turning to pull me into his arms while we waited for the valet. I didn't know I was shaking so badly until his arms warmed my chilled body, and the panic that had consumed me dissipated. I pressed my head against his chest, drinking in his strength. Once the car arrived, he guided me as if I were a child. I guess I resembled one at the moment, as I was silently crying and continued to shake like a leaf. Nicolas buckled me in, and we were on our way.

I replayed the scene over and over in my head. *How much had he heard*, I wondered? Shame threatened to consume me, and I did my best to pull myself together. Nicolas grasped my hand, lacing our fingers yet again, providing me with the only comfort he could at the moment, but it was enough. I latched on to him as if he was a lifesaver, one that would keep me afloat in this sea of emotional turmoil.

"*Ne pleurez pas,* Ieshelle. Don't cry!"

I did my best to control my tears, but there seemed to be an endless supply.

Nicolas soon pulled up into his driveway and hopped out of the car. I got out, following him like a marionette. We walked into the living room, where Nicolas guided me to sit on the couch before heading to the bar. He came back moments later with two tumblers of amber-colored liquor.

"Here—drink this," he instructed.

I shook my head rejecting the offering, unsure if I was capable of swallowing anything at the moment.

"You're in shock. You need this, Ieshelle."

I took the glass from his hand, realizing my own hand was shaking, and took a healthy sip. The liquid was smooth, creating a warm path down my throat into my stomach. I could feel it spreading, as if a generator was radiating waves of heat rapidly throughout my entire body. I actually felt a little better.

"Thank you."

Nicolas emptied his glass and refilled it before sitting next to me on the couch. I took another sip of the amber-colored liquid before placing my glass on the table. Taking a deep breath, I tried once again to pull my frayed nerves together. Nicolas shifted on the couch before coming to kneel before me. I couldn't move. I was trapped by those piercing blue eyes and what I saw reflected there—compassion, understanding, and another emotion I was too afraid to name. His hands were warm as they slid beneath the folds of my dress to grasp my ankle and remove my shoe.

"Tell me, Ieshelle," he said, as he removed the other shoe. He massaged my calves and then ran his hands along the soles of my feet. I couldn't hide the knee-jerking sensation the caress elicited, but Nicolas continued as if nothing had happened, again demanding, "Tell me, Ieshelle."

In the end, I couldn't hide my relief, because I actually wanted to talk about the incident—I *needed* to talk about it. "I met Damien the summer of my eighteenth birthday.

We were still living in Jamaica at the time," I started. "He was on vacation with some friends. I thought he was the most attractive guy I ever had seen—sophisticated, intelligent, and successful. I thought I loved him. After he went home, we talked over the phone for several months, and he came back to visit several times. After six months, he proposed. I knew it was quick, but I thought we were in love. Anyway, he brought me and my mother to Las Vegas, where he was living. After a couple of months, things rapidly disintegrated."

"He and my mother didn't get along, so eventually she moved out, and I stayed with him. That should have been a red flag, but I was too blinded by love. The first time he hit me, I convinced myself it was an accident. We had been arguing, and I threw something at him, so I felt like it was my fault that he struck me, because I started it. The second time he hit me, we got into a brawl. I found him in bed with another woman. She fled when I busted in the bedroom, and he attacked. I knew then that I couldn't stay with him, but he hurt me so bad . . . I had to be careful. He threatened to hurt my mother too. The third incident was the final time."

I paused, remembering that day vividly. Nicolas continued his ministrations, his hands soothing as they continued to drift over my legs. "I told him I was leaving," I explained. "I was pregnant, and I knew that I couldn't raise my child with him—he was too unstable, and I wouldn't allow my baby to witness that. I had also realized that he didn't love me, not really. I planned on being gone before he came home from work, but he arrived early, and I was still packing. I guess he realized it was over, that I really meant it when I said I was leaving and I wasn't coming back. I had never seen him in such a rage. I fought back, which shocked him, as he believed he had taught me to submit after our last altercation. My fighting him seemed to incite his anger, and he pushed me back so hard that I flew through the sliding glass door of the dining room. When I didn't get up, he thought I was faking and even kicked me a couple of times, but I was fighting for consciousness, and when I didn't move and he saw the blood . . . I guess that's when he panicked. He . . . he left. He left me there . . ."

I shook my head, the scene still replaying before me like a movie. "When I woke up, I was lying in a pool of blood. My stomach was cramping, and I had a large piece of glass stuck in my side. I crawled to the phone and dialed 911. By the time I got to the hospital, there was nothing they could do to save the baby. I had lost too much blood." I wrapped my arms around my midsection, feeling that loss all over again.

Nicolas moved swiftly, taking me up in his arms to draw me across his lap so that I was cradled against him. It felt good to let him comfort me, and I wasn't scared to allow him to see my weakened state. He kissed my cheeks, bringing warmth where icy tears had trailed, before moving to kiss my eyes, my brow, and the hollow of my neck. I reached up to cup his cheek, bringing his lips in firm contact with my own. His were warm and coaxing, seeking to draw pleasure. I moved closer to him, straining for more, needing more. I needed him. There—I admitted it to myself. I need him.

"Ieshelle, I don't think this is a good idea," Nicolas whispered, his breathing labored.

Feeling his rejection, I moved to slide from his lap to the couch, but strong arms held me in place.

"Ieshelle, listen to me—you are hurting," Nicolas pointed out. Feeling my face flush with embarrassment, I attempted again to stand, only to have him press my back against the couch with my legs draped across his thighs as he half covered me. "Ieshelle, how could you think I don't want you?" he questioned before snaking his hand out to clasp mine, flush against the hard, bulging erection that filled his pants. "There is nothing I want more than to make love to you, Ieshelle, but that is not what you need tonight."

He released my hand, but I let it linger there, fascinated at his response to me. I thought maybe he had changed his mind about . . .

"Ieshelle, I want you to be sure, because I want everything, *mon ange,* not just your body."

Struck by his honesty, I looked into his intense blue eyes as they bore into my soul. It was as if he could see everything and knew everything. *How had he discovered so much about me and my nature when I was confused about myself?* I knew from the beginning that he was dangerous. He wanted everything—all of me! The only question was, did I trust him enough to submit to his possession?

Twenty-Four

I t took all of my control to maintain my cool, as my emotions were a boiling cauldron beneath the surface. Rage threatened to consume and propel me into a fit of destruction. I held Ieshelle in my arms, offering the comfort I knew she needed, even as I desired to claim her as mine. I longed to wipe the anguish and hurt from her eyes and replace it with the vitality that was there only hours ago. Visions of Ieshelle in Damien's arms continued to play over and over in my head, like a movie on repeat. Initially, I was angry, believing she had used me as a buffer between her and her lover. As I listened to what they were saying, however, wrath caused my vision to go red. I wanted to rip him to pieces. And I would have done so, if not for the sight of Ieshelle, quivering and distraught. The sight had been like being doused with cold water, cooling my fury. She needed me, and her needs came above all else.

I gathered Ieshelle to me, her body stiff and her spine rigid in shock. I did my best to quickly get her out of the hotel. The shot of brandy had put some color back in her cheeks, and she was no longer shaking as if she would blow away in the wind. The tears nearly undid me. I wanted to pound that motherfucker into the ground. *How could he have hurt her like that? How could he have abused her?* She was strong, though. She had recovered, started her own business, and formed a support group for women. Ieshelle had prevailed, but now, she needed comfort. She needed to know she could trust me. It would take all my strength to

D'STARR

contain my passions, but once I developed the plan, I knew it was the right course of action. I could withstand anything for her.

She was draped across my lap, and I wanted to be sure that she understood my intentions. I wasn't quite sure she knew what that entailed. *Hell, I had just figured it out myself.* When I told her I wanted everything, I meant it. I wanted her to be mine, always.

She looked at me for the longest time, her eyes searching, until her hand came up to caress my cheek, urging me closer so that her lips brushed mine. "I understand what you are saying, Nicolas. I trust you," she confessed.

Those words were imprinted on my heart, and I understood the magnitude of what it meant for her to submit. I took her mouth, branding her with my kiss, staking my claim. Ieshelle was my woman. I kissed her again and again, drugging her with passion. She was straining against me, her hands running over my shoulders and back, and I scooped her up to head upstairs to my bedroom. I stood her before my bed and carefully lowered the zipper on the dazzling dress. As it fell to the floor, she stood there in the most erotic undergarments

I had ever seen—a turquoise silk bustier with dainty matching panties. The bustier lifted her breasts in offering and enhanced her small waist and curvy hips. I reached out to skim my fingers along the top where her delectable breasts strained to be contained.

I brought her hands up to my chest, wanting her to undress me as I had undressed her. She moved her hands within my jacket, skimming them across my chest and shoulders until it dropped off and pooled at our feet. Ieshelle removed my tie and unbuttoned my shirt, and once it was completely open, she stepped closer to place a gentle kiss on my collarbone. She placed another just over my heart and then ran her tongue over my nipple, all the while her hands, featherlike in their touch, drifted over my skin as if she were memorizing every inch.

The moment her tongue touched my skin I wanted nothing more than to throw her down on the bed and cover her. But tonight was about her, so I found the strength to withstand her touch. Ieshelle's hands moved to the belt at my waist, which she deftly removed. She unbuttoned my pants, sliding her hands within my black boxers to cup and mold my ass before sliding them past my hips to release my engorged shaft. Her hands skimmed over the head of my cock, causing me to jerk from the sensation. It was too much. I grabbed her hands before my resolve was broken and then bent down and hefted her over my right shoulder.

I let my hands drift over her delectable curves before laying her across the bed, readjusting my boxers before joining her. I had to keep that under wraps if I planned on making it through the night. Ieshelle was seduction personified. I kissed her again, taking her lips over and over before demanding entry into the recesses of her mouth. I started working the fastenings at the front of the bustier, trailing my lips over to the spot just below her ear, tracing the outline of the butterfly's wing with my tongue. She was panting and writhing beneath me, her legs cradling me in abandon.

As I undid the last clasp, her breast sprang free, and the mocha-tipped globes filled my hands. I squeezed, flicking my thumbs over the sensitive buds. Her response was immediate as the soft tissue budded before my eyes. Ieshelle lifted her hips off the bed, grinding against me. I knew what she wanted, but I needed to savor her, to worship her as she deserved. I bent my head, taking her left nipple deep within my mouth, while fondling the other. I skimmed my hand between us to slide beneath the band of her panties, delving into the ebony curls that covered her sex.

Ieshelle bucked then, the sensation sweeping through her as I slid my fingers along her clit and across her channel. She was wet, her essence covering my fingers completely. I took her other nipple deep within my mouth as I plunged a finger briefly within her core. She was tight, the muscles contracting around me, as I continued to stroke her, pumping in and out, mimicking the act I yearned to perform. She was close. I could feel her body tightening, as her hands no longer roamed across my back and shoulders but were merely holding me to her as she strained for completion. I pumped once, then twice, massaging her bud with each sweep, scraping her nipple with my teeth before soothing the sting with my kiss. Ieshelle erupted in my arms, my name upon her lips as she fell over the cliff into ecstasy.

I continued to stroke her lazily as I trailed kisses across her abdomen, taking a break only to slide the dainty panties from her hips.

I rolled the thigh-high stockings down her legs, placing kisses along the exposed skin, until she was completely naked before me. Her legs were long and shapely, I noted, as I draped them over my forearms. I bent my head, kissing her inner thigh. I watched her as her hands roamed over her stomach to cradle her breasts, seeking my kiss, my touch, her hips thrusting the air in expectation. She was bewitching and her fragrance permeated the air, a siren's call I could not ignore.

I leaned forward, running my tongue deep within her folds, laving her bud over and over again before sinking my tongue within her core. Ieshelle was riding me, her hips rocking to and fro. I lifted her even higher, sliding my hands beneath her rear as I suckled her bud over and over, before licking her from clit to her core and back again. I could feel the passion coiling within her again, attuned to her reaction to my assault. She tightened her hold on my shoulders, and I repeated the move over and over until I heard her cry out. I applied just the right amount of pressure, my tongue massaging her sensitive flesh until she tumbled over the edge once again. The orgasm swept through her relentlessly until she was pleading with me to stop, her hips bucking and legs shaking uncontrollably. It was glorious.

I pulled her to me so that her back was to my chest, my burgeoning erection nestled against her rounded derriere. I held her as the tremors of her orgasmic aftermath continued to rack her body, and I kissed her temple and nuzzled her neck. Eventually, she quieted, and I knew sleep claimed her as her breathing became deep and even. I lay awake for what must have been hours, using every mantra I knew to quiet the raging desire within me. Ieshelle was ecstasy in my arms, her body molding to mine. I had found what I had been missing—my other half. I was walking a tightrope of control the urge to flip her over and plunge deep into the depths of her sex, bringing her to orgasm yet again, assaulted me. Her scent clung to me. I tasted her in my mouth and wanted her again, but my will was strong. I continued to hold her until daylight began to filter through the window, and then I eased from the bed. I needed to make some arrangements this morning, and I would see to Ieshelle's needs. I hoped that seeing to her desires would eventually satisfy my own.

Twenty-Five

I rolled over, swamped by cushions and the delicious scent of Nicolas. *Nicolas! Oh, my God, it wasn't a dream. Everything . . . it was real!* I ran my hand along my neck, remembering his touch, his kiss. He had given me such pleasure and had comforted me when I needed it most, without taking anything in return. Never had a man given me such a selfless gift or worshiped me with his touch, his mouth. I rolled over to stare at those gorgeous blue eyes, trying not to blush with the new intimacy.

He leaned over, placing a chaste kiss against my lips. "Good morning."

He tasted of mint, reminding me that I needed to clean up. I felt like my face was on fire. How could I be so bashful when we had shared such a mutually gratifying experience. But it wasn't mutual, was it?

As if he could read my mind, he rolled from the bed, stating simply, "My pleasure is your pleasure, *mon ange*. You can shower while I finish breakfast. I left some things in there for you." He pointed toward a door that I assumed was the bathroom.

"Thank you," I said, pulling the sheet around me. I felt silly for being embarrassed about my nudity, but I felt like a schoolgirl again. I walked into the bathroom and was pleased to find a new white T-shirt, blue cotton Bermuda shorts, bra, panties, and flip- flops. There was also a new toothbrush on the counter next to a tube of toothpaste. I checked the sizes, and everything was perfect, from the shirt and short sizes to the flip-flops. *How had he done that? Better yet, when did he have the time to get all of this?* I stepped into the shower quickly, as the smell of bacon permeated the air and my stomach rumbled in response.

When I emerged from the bedroom, the house was silent. I noted the time on the clock was well past eight and wondered where the training staff was. Nicolas was usually up and had completed his first session of training by the time I arrived, so where was everyone today? I walked down the stairs, the smell of fresh coffee, added to the already tempting aroma of bacon, luring me.

Nicolas was in the kitchen a towel slung around his shoulders, the T-shirt he wore clinging to him in places but not due to sweat. He must have showered too. He turned then, as if he sensed my arrival. "Perfect timing—the food is ready. Have a seat," he instructed.

"Where is everyone?" I asked as I took a seat at the table.

"Day off."

"Day off?" I repeated. "But won't that put you behind with your training?"

"No, because I will be working out, just in a different way."

A blush spread across my cheeks at what his words implied.

Then I thought, *Shit, I can't afford to take a day off!* There was too much going on, and I needed to see my mother today.

"Eat your breakfast, Ieshelle," Nicolas directed. "We will talk afterwards."

I was still amazed at how he did that. I sat down, noting there was a carafe of orange juice and a basket of croissants on the table. Nicolas placed what looked like spinach and potato frittata, fresh fruit, and two strips of bacon in front of me before sitting across the table with a plate holding four times the amount of food on mine.

"I have some coffee on, but it's not ready yet."

The food was very good—Nicolas, surprisingly, was a great cook. Once both of our plates were clear, and we were sipping our second cup of coffee, Nicolas started. "I called your office and told them that you wouldn't be in today. If there are any emergent calls, they will contact this number or your cell."

"You did *what?* You had no right to do that!"

His tone was unwavering as he responded, "I know, but you need it, just like you need me."

I stared at him in silence, unable to speak past the knot lodged in my throat.

He continued, watching me constantly. "But you are not ready to face it, so I'm going to help you."

"What about you?" I asked, wishing I could take the words back as soon as they'd left my mouth, because I wasn't sure I wanted to hear the answer.

"Ieshelle, I have made it no secret that I want you. I have from the very beginning. I enjoy being with you. You are a phenomenal woman."

"But . . . you didn't kiss me again after that first day . . . well, until last night, but still—"

"I was trying to respect the fact that you were determined to keep our relationship professional."

"That's a lie! If you wanted our relationship to remain professional, you wouldn't have demanded me as your therapist."

"I told you before that I would not lie to you and there would be no secrets between us. All you had to do was ask me my motives for having you as my therapist, and I would have told you."

"What are your motives, Nicolas?" I asked tentatively.

"I wanted you with me. I wanted time to get to know you. The objective was to seduce you, but as the days went on... something changed," he admitted. "Before last night, I had every intention of keeping our relationship professional until my arm was healed and our contract completed. That was before . . ."

Reminded of the embarrassing encounter with Damien, I got up from the table and headed for the bedroom. *I have to get my clothes,* I thought. *Shit! How did I let him see me so weak and defeated?* Before I made it to the doorway, his strong arms engulfed me. I attempted to free myself, but his voice was a soothing caress in my ear.

"Be still, Ieshelle." His lips pressed against the side of my neck. His touched warmed my blood, and I stopped struggling against his grasp. *God, what he did to me!* "Don't run from me, *ange,* for you will force me to pursue you, when all I want is to let you come to me."

"I don't know what you want from me. I don't understand, Nicolas."

Twenty-Six

I turned Ieshelle around to look into her eyes, and tears glistened there. Damn! I hated seeing her cry. I couldn't sleep last night, thinking of the repercussions of our encounter. After everything Damien had done to her, I knew she was leery of letting anyone get close. She was probably scared she would make the same mistake. I had to prove to her that what was developing between us was not a mistake. As I watched her sleep last night, her face completely relaxed, I realized I would never grow tired of looking at her or hearing her laugh. She was what I had been looking for, even though I hadn't realized it. Somehow, I had to make her see that what was developing between us was real.

I brushed my finger along her cheek. "Ieshelle, last night put us on fast forward. I'm sorry for that, because I know you are not ready for this next level. Hell, I'm not sure if I'm ready, but I am willing to try."

"Nicolas, you . . . you sound as if . . ." She grasped my hand, her slim fingers circling my wrist.

I stepped closer as I tried to convey my intentions. "Ieshelle, I'm not going anywhere."

"Nicolas? How could you—" she asked, shaking her head in disbelief.

I pulled her into my arms kissing her, effectively ending her question. I wanted her to relax and not panic at the thought of being in a relationship. My desire was to go slow, but time was not on my side. I had little over a week before I would return to New Mexico, if Dr. Marcley gave the okay. I trailed my lips against her brow, just holding her. I could feel the tension slowly ease from her shoulders as she laid her head against my chest, her arms circling my waist.

"I don't usually take days off," she confessed, "Unless it has something to do with my mother, Eden Rose, or DIVAS."

"I figured as much. To be honest, I don't usually take days off from training, which is why I went running this morning while you were still sleeping." She pinched my side, making me chuckle. "We could go for a walk if you'd like. It's not too hot yet," I suggested.

She paused, and I thought she was going to refuse, but then she responded, "I would like that."

◆ ◆ ◆

I took her hand in mine as we walked along one of the many trails in the neighborhood. The day was perfect, the clouds provided excellent cover, and an occasional breeze helped to combat the desert heat. The pleasant weather had the neighborhood bustling as people were out in abundance taking advantage. It had been a while since I just took a walk and observed the world around me. I was always busy. If I wasn't training or attending a promotional event, I was preparing for the upcoming movie. It seemed that time was never on my side, a fact that weighed on my mind, considering my new circumstances. My arm was getting stronger every day, and I knew that long before Ieshelle or I was ready, I would have to go back to New Mexico.

Ieshelle's voice pulled me back from my thoughts. "You have a beautiful neighborhood."

"Thank you. It's only one of the houses I own, but it does have the most pleasant and well-thought-out locality." We walked a little further before I asked something I was curious about after her disclosure last night. "Does your mother still live here?"

She faltered a step before recovering, her grip on my hand tightening slightly as if she were drawing strength from me.

"She is still here in Las Vegas, but she suffered a ruptured brain aneurysm two months ago and is still in the hospital."

"I'm sorry to hear that, Ieshelle." I brought our joined hands to rest over my heart, running my thumb over her knuckles unconsciously. "Are you an only child?"

"No . . . I mean, yes." She took a deep breath before continuing. "I had a younger brother, Antonio, but he was killed when he was five. That was before we left Jamaica. It was one of the reasons I was so ready to leave when Damien offered to help me and my mother relocate. We could start over."

"I see." I brushed my lips across her knuckles. "Both of my parents still live in Canada. Nicolette is contemplating moving to California. She wants to open a restaurant somewhere in the wine country. She already has a successful restaurant here called Dragonfly. But you probably know that already—you two seemed to have hit it off."

"She's nice; it's hard not to like her. I couldn't believe it when she told me she owned the restaurant. I love the food there, and they have great drinks."

"I'm only too happy to help her realize her dreams."

"You financed her restaurant?"

"Yes, does that surprise you?"

"No," she responded thoughtfully. "Nicolette is an excellent cook. Anything she takes on will be a success. You're not bad yourself, you know."

"Why, thank you, *mademoiselle*." We continued walking. I was truly enjoying the time with Ieshelle. I had learned a lot about her. But I wanted more. I wanted it all. Without preamble, I asked, "Who is Eden Rose?"

"Dr. Eden Rose Montgomery—well, Montgomery-Preston now. She's my best friend, really, more like my sister. We met when we were eight years old. Her family was vacationing in Jamaica. We hit it off and kept in touch after that. She was the one who took me in after I left Damien."

"I'm glad you have someone like her. It must have been hard finding yourself again after experiencing something so tragic."

"It was, but Eden Rose and my mother helped me through it. Eden Rose shared with me her love of medicine, and I found my purpose in physical therapy. Through helping others restore their health, I was able to heal myself. I also started the women's support group that provided a way for me to help those who were in similar circumstances."

We continued to talk about our families, our professions, and our hopes and dreams. I needed to arm myself with everything I could in order to help Ieshelle accept our relationship. She was able to function—even thrive, to an extent—but the wounds were still there and had not healed completely. One wrong move, and it would be like reopening the insecurities of her past. I just hoped this leap would not be too much too soon. I had to tread carefully if I wanted to win the ultimate prize.

Twenty-Seven

N icolas and I walked and talked for hours, until the sun was beaming overhead and we retreated back to the house. I learned that Nicolas had not always been an MMA fighter but had originally trained as a boxer and wrestler in his teens before switching to mixed martial arts. His mother, Anna, and his father, Jean, had been married for over fifty years. His father had been a mill worker and his mother a local school teacher. The first thing Nicolas wanted to do when he won his first major fight, he told me, was to buy his parents a new house. But they wouldn't hear of it, so he paid off, and renovated their farm. Now, his father worked the land, providing fruits and vegetables at the local market.

Nicolas talked about his plans for the future. He was part owner of Zen Studios, the gym where he trained while here; the main gym was in New Mexico. His trainer, Frank, was the majority shareholder. Nicolas wanted to be a part of the project because he knew the gym could be a safe haven for young boys and girls. It had been a way for him to escape a life of poverty and a dead-end job at a pulp mill. He'd started acting classes and was scheduled to start shooting his first movie after the rematch fight with Mark Hiden. I could see him as the next martial arts hero—he was sexy as hell.

When we returned to the house, we fixed a light lunch— turkey sandwiches on whole wheat with salads. We moved around each other with an easy familiarity, which made it hard to believe we had only really just met.

Nicolas was an amazing man. He scared me with his honesty—with him, there was no pretense. Maybe he scared me because he forced me to be honest with myself. He was slowly forcing me to see that I had fallen in love with him. He hadn't spoken about it earlier, saying I wasn't ready yet. Maybe he was right. After Damien, I hadn't trusted any man or let anyone get close—until Nicolas.

After we finished cleaning up the kitchen for the second time that day, I suggested, "I think we should complete your conditioning exercises and tissue massage so that you will not be so off schedule."

Nicolas nodded in agreement and headed toward the rehab room. I followed him, only to remember I didn't have my bag.

"Don't worry," he said. "There should be some of the oil you use on the table there. I picked up some after the first session so that I could use it when you weren't here . . . and besides, it reminded me of you."

"Okay," I responded breathlessly as Nicolas removed his shirt to lie face down on the massage table. I poured a small amount of the oil onto my palm and then applied it liberally to his left shoulder and arm. He was a magnificent specimen of man, beautiful not only on the outside but full of depth and character. He flipped over, and I started the process again. I had completed the massage and conditioning exercises, but I wasn't yet ready to end the session. I let my hands trail over his chest, smoothing the oil there, tracing the Chinese symbols tattooed on his right pectoral muscle. "What does this mean?" I asked.

"'The more we sweat in training, the less we bleed in battle.' It's an old Chinese proverb."

Maybe that's why he trains so hard, I thought. I let my hands drift over his chest, tracing the tattoo of the tiger that started on his left pec to drift down his side. It looked so real—the artist had done a superb job with color and shading, giving it a 3-D appearance. There were three slashes that appeared as if the tiger had struck through the flesh of Nicolas's chest in an attempt to escape from within. The tiger's face was just visible within the slashes, and familiar blue eyes peered out. I let my hands drift over his body, fascinated with the way his muscles contracted beneath my feather-light touch. Desire burned in my stomach. I wanted him . . . *but was I ready to accept everything he was offering?*

My hands stilled as I felt his heartbeat beneath my palm. His hand covered mine, startling me so that I looked to his face. I didn't know how long I had been standing there, but his expression was watchful, as if he was reading my thoughts again.

"Come on. I'll take you to see your mother, and then we can stop by your house to pick up some of your things."

I looked at him questioningly, wondering exactly what he meant. *Were we in a relationship or just lovers? He said that he wanted me, but what did that mean? Did he want me now but maybe not tomorrow?* I didn't know. I could feel my throat tighten as panic crept in.

What am I doing?

"Breathe, Ieshelle, just breathe. I'm not going anywhere."

He had made that very statement before.

"What does that mean?" I asked. "I don't know what to think or how to feel. I'm . . . I'm . . ."

Before I knew what was happening, I was sitting across Nicolas's lap, and his lips were covering mine. The kiss was a command, and

I lost myself in him. *Nicolas understands me better than I understand myself.* I wanted this; I wanted him to kiss me, but I had been too scared to initiate it.

"Ieshelle, you have to learn to trust yourself again," he whispered against my lips. "Only then will you let yourself trust me completely."

I stared into his eyes, sea-blue pools that hid nothing from me. His mouth was inches from my own. I did the only thing I could—I closed the distance between us and kissed him back. Where his kiss was commanding, I explored. I leisurely sampled his lips as my hands wandered across his shoulders and chest. Desire, never far from the surface when in his presence, exploded in my chest; an unrelenting flame consumed me from within. I could feel my head clouding with passion, and desire thickened my blood as it flowed throughout every cell, concentrating within my womanhood. A steady pulse beat causing my sex to throb. I groaned in frustration, needing more contact. There were too many clothes in the way.

Nicolas was the one to break the kiss. I stared at him in confusion, but he only smiled at me reassuringly before placing a quick peck on my lips. "Come on. We need to go see your mother before it gets too late."

I nodded consent, knowing he was right, but feeling the aftereffects of our kiss—my blood seemed to swelter beneath my skin. I brushed my fingers against my lips, still in shock at my response to him. The tissue was slightly swollen, and I could only assume that I looked like I had been thoroughly ravished. Nicolas smiled then, as if he had read my mind yet again. His eyes sparkled devilishly. *I really am in trouble.*

Twenty-Eight

The hospital was active when we arrived, the sound of monitors humming and nurses moving in and out of rooms. I hated the antiseptic smell, but I would endure anything for Ieshelle. She was very quiet and had been since we arrived. The nurse, Carmen, was leaving the room as we reached the door and informed Ieshelle that her mother was resting.

"You've come at a good time," Carmen said. "The doctors are making their rounds."

The name Sophie Jones was printed neatly outside the door. I ran my hand up and down Ieshelle's back, gently offering support. She paused a moment before entering, as if she was composing herself.

Sophie was sitting up; the head of the bed was slightly elevated. She looked at me curiously as I followed Ieshelle into the room. She had the same caramel-colored eyes as her daughter, but other than that, Ieshelle bore little resemblance to her mother. Her mother's complexion was much darker, her skin resembling milk chocolate. She had strong cheekbones, a distinguished nose, and a demure mouth. She seemed regal, reminding me of a queen.

"Momma, how are you today?" Ieshelle asked.

Sophie lifted her left hand and tilted it from left to right. I noticed a stiffness around her mouth and jaw, evidence of her continued disability. Ieshelle sat on the bed next to her and grabbed her hand. "Your physical therapist said you were able to sit at the side of the bed and hold your own weight yesterday during therapy. That's a great accomplishment!"

Her mother nodded slightly and then turned to look at me. Her eyes held an undeniable wisdom. I could feel her sizing me up. Ieshelle looked to me then, uncertainty written on her face. "Momma, this is Nicolas . . . Nicolas St. Pierre, he's my . . . my . . ."

"Ms. Jones," I quickly interjected, suspecting the cause of Ieshelle's doubt. I myself was finding it difficult to put into words the significance of our relationship, the words "girlfriend" or "significant other" too paltry to describe the depth of emotion that Ieshelle evoked within me. I opted on the truth as my only recourse, even if Ieshelle wasn't ready to hear it. "I plan to be a permanent part of Ieshelle's life—that is, if she will accept me." Up until this point, I had only informed Ieshelle that I wanted her. Sophie studied my face intently before smiling and nodding in understanding. Ieshelle looked at me in astonishment. Her reaction let me know just how difficult a challenge this would be. Ieshelle didn't believe me; she didn't believe in us. Not yet.

"Stubborn!" The raspy, faint word was like a shout within the hospital room, and both Ieshelle and I focused on Sophie's mouth. She repeated it with more force. "Stubborn!"

"Momma, when did you start talking again?" Ieshelle asked. I could hear the tears in her voice, and I stepped closer, placing my hand on her shoulder reassuringly. She reached up unconsciously, her hand covering my own, seeking the comfort I was willing to provide.

"Today," her mother responded.

Ieshelle and her mother talked more about her progress and what the speech therapist had planned, now that she was speaking again. Sophie shared what she accomplished in occupational therapy today as well. Ieshelle told her mother that Sheba, her dog, was due to come home from the vet soon. She talked about Eden Rose and her new husband, Jacob, and that she suspected there would be a baby soon. They laughed together, her mother chuckling softly. It was captivating to see them together. I could imagine how they must have interacted when Sophie was not ailing. Suddenly, they both turned to me expectantly. I had missed something.

Sophie smiled. "I asked what you do for a living."

"I am a fighter," I responded. "Mixed martial arts."

"How did you and Shelly meet?"

Shelly, huh? I looked toward Ieshelle teasingly.

She rolled her eyes before responding. "He was injured in one of his last fights. The agency is providing his rehab."

"Mmmm. She is the best, Nicolas. You are in good hands."

I looked at Ieshelle once again, recognizing just how right Sophie was. Nicolette warned me that I was vulnerable, and she was right. *But I don't have to be,* I realized. I was in "good hands" with Ieshelle, not only as it related to my rehab but also my heart.

Just then there was a knock outside the door before the nurse poked her head in, saying that the doctor was here and would be in momentarily. I moved toward the door, intending to step out into the hall and give them some privacy during the visit, but Ieshelle latched onto my hand, and her mother started shaking her head no. Sophie held out her hand, and I clasped it to me, placing a chaste kiss across her knuckle, pleased to be accepted so easily.

A short, rotund Indian man entered, with two taller Caucasian assistants behind him. He greeted Ieshelle and her mother warmly and introduced himself to me as Dr. Harish and the assistants as his fellows. He then discussed Sophie's chart and the current plan.

"You've made substantial progress since your admission," he told Sophie, "But you still need extensive rehabilitation. You will need to consider transfer to a rehabilitation facility so you can continue physical and occupational therapy." The transfer could be as soon as next Wednesday, depending on approval from the insurance company. When he asked if we had any questions, Ieshelle led him toward the door, saying she wanted to ask him something outside, which left me alone with her mother.

I took up Ieshelle's seat on the bed, knowing already what I needed to say—I might never get another chance alone with her. "Ms. Jones—"

Immediately, she started shaking her head no. "Sophie," she whispered, her voice soft and strained.

"Ms. Sophie"—she smiled at my adding 'Ms.' in front of her name—"I love your daughter. I have come to realize that, and I think she—no, I know she loves me too . . . only she is too scared to accept that the love I have for her is unconditional."

She nodded in understanding. "Stubborn."

"Yes, she can be, but I know she has been hurt also."

She looked surprised that I knew and then shook her head.

"Damien," she whispered.

"I met him, and I have to admit, I wanted to pound his face into the pavement. That was even before I found out what he had done to Ieshelle. More important, though, is that Ieshelle has not completely healed from the experience. I can only pray that by being patient, I can show her that she can trust in my love for her and in the love she has for me. I hope that I can ask your blessing to pursue Ieshelle."

Sophie's face revealed nothing as she contemplated all that I had shared. I continued talking, as I felt a need to further plead my case. "I am from St. Isadore, Canada. My mother and father both still reside there and have been married for over fifty years. I own a house here in Las Vegas and one in New Mexico. I have a twin sister and no children. Ieshelle is safe with me. I would never hurt her. Her happiness comes before my own, always."

She was still watching me quietly, and I felt compelled to fill the silence, I was about to start talking again when she squeezed my hand. I looked into her familiar eyes and saw what I needed most—approval and acceptance.

Ieshelle returned then and explained that she had wanted to review the latest MRI results with Dr. Harish and provide him with the contact numbers to several facilities in which the agency provided rehab. She worked Sophie through a series of conditioning exercises, and when her mother started to yawn, Ieshelle decided it might be time for us to go. She kissed and hugged Sophie, and I kissed her cheek as well giving her a hug. As I moved to pull back, Sophie held me tighter and whispered in my ear, "Thank you for taking care of my baby. Don't give up on her."

I realized that Sophie was skeptical about her recovery. The words held finality that I didn't want to contemplate, and I was afraid that

Ieshelle might not be strong enough for their meaning. I would have to be strong enough to carry her if she needed me to; I had to be.

Twenty-Nine

I was happy and scared at the same time. I had learned a lot about Nicolas, including something that had been weighing on my mind—his intentions. I was glad that he had not said the word "marriage." I was still trying to come to terms that he was my man. *My man? When did I start claiming him as such?* I don't know, but it is irrevocably true—Nicolas is mine!

I thought about the doctor's comment that my mother was ready to go to a rehabilitation center. She'd spoken today, and I realized that I hadn't heard her voice since before her hospitalization. I wiped at my eyes, taking small, even breaths in an attempt to soothe the emotions that were swirling within me. Energy pulsed throughout my body; I felt wired. Normally, when I felt revved up like this, I would clean my whole house, take a spin on my bike, or cook a big meal.

"Are you hungry?" I asked Nicolas as we pulled into my driveway.

"Yeah, why, what's up?"

"Come on," I instructed as I got out of the car and unlocked the front door to the house. The colors that filled the interior were bold and bright, just like my personality. The living room had bright yellow walls and white furniture with black accents. Yellow and red pillows were scattered on the couch. A yellow, red, black, and white color-block throw rug covered the center of the floor, with a black circular glass coffee table in the center. There were matching tables at each end of the couch and love seat. A picture depicting a butterfly with coordinating colors hung on the wall behind the couch and on either side of the fifty- five-inch flat-screen television. I set my purse on the coffee table and headed for the kitchen, instructing Nicolas to follow me. "I'm going to cook dinner for you," I announced.

I thought about the ingredients in the fridge and cabinets, planning what I would make. "Go ahead and look around," I told him. "It'll take me forty-five minutes, tops. I'll get things started and then give you a full tour if you like."

"Is there anything I can help you with?"

He is so thoughtful. "No, I have it under control. Go ahead and explore." I waved my hand to shoo him away as I entered my favorite room in the house. I loved to cook. I flipped on the radio as I kicked off my shoes. The sound of one of the local DJ's talking filled the air. I switched instead to one of my favorite reggae-ton CDs, and as I looked through the cabinets, pantry, and the fridge, I realized that I needed to go shopping. There would be nothing spectacular tonight, but I could put together a sensible meal.

I still couldn't believe Nicolas wanted us to attempt a relationship, especially when he was leaving for New Mexico in a couple of weeks. *Would a long-distance relationship work?* My life was here; his life was between here and New Mexico, but his fights could take him anywhere.

He was right; I wasn't ready for this. I took a deep breath, remembering Nicolas's instruction from earlier: '*Breathe, just breathe, Ieshelle. Go slow.*' But how could I go slow when everything in me was screaming at me to jump him at the first chance. It was more than desire that was riding me, more than lust. I genuinely liked him. He was a family man. He loved his parents and his sister and was willing to support them. He had a dominant personality but was considerate. It was alluring. He had seduced me into sharing all of my deepest secrets—and I felt better. Lighter. I felt as if the wounds were healing this time instead of just being covered with a bandage.

He was just as vulnerable as I was—I remembered the tension that had filled him when he discussed his injury. It had to have been daunting for him to be defeated—forced to submit or risk his arm being broken. Maybe I could help him as he had helped me. I thought about what my mother said—if I didn't take a risk, I could end up all alone. Eden Rose had taken a risk on Jacob and look at her now. Happily married.

Thoughts of Eden Rose and Jacob encouraged me. It hadn't been easy for them in the beginning, but they worked it out. Love prevailed. But was I in love with Nicolas? I took another deep breath and decided to relax and follow Nicolas's lead.

Thirty

I walked around the living room while Ieshelle was working in the kitchen. I could hear the clanging sound of pots and pans banging around, just before the air filled with Reggae-ton music. Ieshelle was a mélange of personalities. Pictures of her homeland, mother, and brother lined the mantel of the fireplace. There were also pictures of the beautiful redheaded Eden Rose and a dark-haired gentleman that I assumed was her husband, Jacob. He looked familiar, but I couldn't place his face. Tiny butterflies of coordinating colors were placed around the room—a red one here, a yellow one there.

I wandered into the dining room, which was somewhat a continuance of the living room except the walls were red with white trim. The décor was a little less contemporary and more country kitchen, with a white dinette set and matching armoire. Red and yellow flowers in a blue vase were on the table, and a yellow, white, and blue color-block throw rug was on the floor.

The armoire held cerulean blue crystal dishes, with matching crystal goblets embellished with tiny butterflies around the rim. Small white butterflies adorned the vase in the middle of the table, and several pictures hung on the walls with blue backgrounds and white butterflies of varying shapes taking flight. The kitchen was adjacent to the dining room, and I saved that for last. As I continued my exploration, I discovered a washroom off the living room that was colored in black, white, and red. There was a huge red butterfly on the black throw rug, with tiny matching butterflies on the soap dish and black hand towels. I discovered a closet in the hall beneath the stairs and a sitting room off to the right.

This room was in sharp contrast to the living and dining rooms and gave me insight to another side of Ieshelle's character. Everything in this room was dainty. The carpet was pale lavender, and a soft mint material covered a cherry wood Victorian couch, love seat, and arm chair. A cherry wood coffee table and end tables were situated appropriately within the room, and over the fireplace was a painting of Sophie in her younger days—she was even more beautiful then. Her caramel eyes cast a knowing glance and glowed from within. Period lamps were perched on the end tables and bright lavender throw pillows adorned with mint green butterflies littered the couch, love seat, and arm chair.

I closed the door and ventured into the next room, which turned out to be a study. It had a tropical feel to it. The colors were soft browns with heavy mahogany furniture and tan paint. Filled bookshelves lined two walls. There was a computer, fax machine, and printer on the large desk that stood before a huge bay window. I looked for the butterflies here and almost missed them. They were intricately carved into the wood scrolling of the desk, chairs and couches in the room.

I headed back to the kitchen, the delicious aromas beckoning me. Ieshelle was a sight. She wore a fuchsia apron and was gyrating to hip-hop music as she fluttered around the kitchen. This room was a menagerie of tropical colors—blue, green, yellow, white, orange. The countertops and matching island were covered in intricate mosaic tile and evidenced the skill of the craftsman. If I looked just right, it appeared as if butterflies were fluttering around. The clear glass doors of the cabinets displayed festive dinner and drinkware. The table in the breakfast nook was fascinating. Butterflies of various species were displayed beneath the glass, along with the same fluttering butterfly mosaic pattern that was found on the countertop. I inhaled deeply, my mouth watering from the savory aromas permeating the air. I said I was hungry, but now that I smelled the food, I felt like I was starving.

"Go wash up; food is almost done," she instructed, her accent more evident as she continued to look into a pot on the stove while gesturing to me with a wooden spoon. She looked adorable and sexy as hell. From my angle, the apron hid the shorts she was wearing, so it appeared that all she had on was the ruffled protective wear, for she had shucked the sandals so her feet were bare. The bright electric-blue-colored nails of her toes caught my eye.

"Yes, *mon ange*," I responded before heading to the washroom. When I returned, Ieshelle was plating the food and gestured for me to have a seat. The plate she set before me caused my stomach to rumble in anticipation.

"I wasn't sure if you liked Caribbean food, so I kept it simple. Brown rice with black beans, pepper shrimp, and baked plantains. There is rum punch in the pitcher on the table and fresh fruit with cream for dessert."

"How did you fix all of this in forty-five minutes?" I asked. "Well, I have to be honest—the beans are from a can, but everything else was fairly simple to cook."

"I'm impressed." I poured us some of the rum punch, and we ate companionably. I was still processing everything that I had learned about her through touring the house. Her house was a home! Each room was a peek into the depths of the woman that she was. I wanted to know every facet of her—everything, all her hopes, every dream, every desire.

"You bought this house after you separated from Damien, didn't you?" I asked. She looked up from her plate, surprise evident in her eyes. She didn't seem to realize how transparent she was. I only had to pay attention. "It was the butterflies that gave it away," I explained.

"How . . . could you know there is significance to the butterflies?"

"I listen to you, not just to the words that come from your mouth, Ieshelle, but the way you move, the energy you exude. You love this house. How long did it take you to decorate?"

"Two and a half years," she whispered. "It took me two years to purge myself of Damien, to heal. Or at least I thought I had healed but . . . Eden Rose is my best friend, and I never told her the meaning of the artwork. She asked, but I dodged her questions. Finally, she gave up asking, but every birthday she gives me something adorned with a butterfly. They morph—they start out from something not as desirable or pretty and morph into a beautiful creature."

"Is that how you see yourself?"

"Not who I am but who I hope to be. That is, until . . ."

"Until what, Ieshelle?" I wondered if she was closer than I thought to accepting our future together. I had my answer with her response.

"Until I met you, Nicolas. How is it that you know me so well? Better than I know myself?"

I walked around the table and pulled her to her feet—I heard the need in her voice and answered her call. "I know, Ieshelle, because I see me in you, if that makes sense." I ran my hand over my head. This might not have been the best time to talk about this, but I needed to share something of myself so that she would understand. "I have never been in love, Ieshelle. I never let anyone get too close. It wasn't because I was hurt in the past, and it wasn't because my parents didn't have a happy marriage. In fact, they are the only reason that I know what true love is. I have always been a loner. Other than Nicolette and my trainers, I consider very few people as friends."

"Then how do you know? How do you know what you feel for me is l-l-love?"

I stepped closer to her, taking her into my arms, "Ieshelle, I know that I love you because your happiness means more to me than my own. Because the only thing I can think about is chasing away the pain and fear from the depths of your eyes and replacing it with joy and love. Love . . . love that is solid, that you can lean on . . . love that you will not be afraid of."

She rested her head against my chest. I wasn't sure if I'd gone too far, too fast. Shit! I knew she wasn't ready for this. I felt her slide her hands up and down my back before she squeezed me tightly in a hug. I picked her up and headed into the living room where I sat on the couch and placed her in my lap. She relaxed against me, her hands running gently over my chest as her breath fanned my neck.

Thirty-One

I reclined against Nicolas, listening to the beat of his heart, trying to settle the butterflies attacking my stomach. He loves me. This man loves me and is unafraid to say it. Trouble was, I felt the same, but the words stuck in my throat. Still, it was okay with him that I didn't say it right back. He was willing to wait for me to . . . to what? To stop being afraid. He knows that I am scared. *Why? Why am I so afraid to explore these feelings between us?* I know I am not scared that he will turn out like Damien; he is nothing like Damien. *So what is it?* I realized then that I needed to go with my feelings, and if I wasn't able to say the words, I could show him.

I sat up to look into Nicolas's watchful eyes. He was so observant; maybe he could see what I could not yet bring myself to confess. I stood up, never breaking eye contact, to look at him— really look at him. He wore denim jeans and a black polo shirt that stretched across his chest, the material delineating his muscular shoulders. He could be one of those sexy male apparel models. He was built but not body-builder bulky. Nicolas was magnificent, like a Greek god, and he loved me!

I unbuttoned the shorts I was wearing, sliding the material past my thighs to pool at my feet. I then lifted my T-shirt up and over my head, tossing it behind me before straddling his legs. Next was the bra, which rapidly joined the growing pile of clothes. His eyes flared with awareness and swept over my exposed flesh like a caress. I slid my hands beneath his shirt and ran it up over his chest. He pulled it off and tossed it over my shoulder before grasping my hips, bringing me in closer contact with his groin.

The wave of pleasure was momentarily disorienting as my core was pressed firmly against his straining erection. I couldn't help grinding my hips against him again and again, exploring the sensation further. I moved my hands up his chest, memorizing the hard planes, languishing in the feel of skin beneath my fingertips. I looked into his eyes before leaning in to run my tongue along the seam of his lips. My hands came up to frame his face. I kissed him then, a brief melding of our lips before I traced his mouth once again with my tongue. His only response was a flaring of his nostrils, which was testament to his control as he allowed me to explore his body. All I really wanted was for him to lose his steely restraint.

I trailed my lips along his jaw before using my tongue to trace the shell of his ear. I took the lobe in between my teeth and gently grazed the skin before licking the area again to soothe the sting. He groaned deep in his chest, but his hands remained clasped to my hips. I trailed my tongue from the spot just beneath his ear, along the pulse in his neck, applying tiny nips here and there but always soothing the area with a kiss or a flick of my tongue afterward. His breathing came in short pants, and I felt rewarded with his response, but it wasn't enough. I kissed the hollow above his collarbone, sliding my hands along his flank. I trailed my left hand up to grasp his neck and then leaned down to run my tongue over his peaked nipple. The small bud was firm against my tongue, and I flicked the sensitive flesh over and over before sucking the peak. I remembered his lips against my breast and a wave of desire fanned the flames running through me. My nipples puckered of their own accord at the memory, and I groaned my own frustration, needing more.

Nicolas's heartbeat pounded in my ears, matching my own. He continued to exhibit monumental control as I explored and tasted him at will. His manhood strained against the confines of his jeans, begging to be released from imprisonment. My hand brushed over the burning heat of his erection, and the gesture meant to tempt his response caused him to jump, his breath catching and his stomach muscles curling. I worked the button free before sliding the zipper down slowly. I continued to fan butterfly soft kisses across his chest until his sex finally sprang free and fell into my hands. I pushed my hand under the fabric covering him to grasp his manhood, glorying in the feel of his heat.

"Ieshelle . . ." Nicolas whispered, his voice strained with tension as he grasped my wrist.

I looked up then, and our eyes locked once again. I leaned forward to brush my lips across his chin, the side of his jaw, before I hovered over his lips, smiling seductively. I wanted him. He wrought from me all of the wanton emotions that I thought were beyond me. He became so distracted that he didn't realize he had released my wrist. I delighted in the freedom, but it wasn't enough. I flicked my tongue across his lips, pressing quick kisses intermittently. I whispered against his lips, "Set me free, Nicolas," and I knelt at his feet.

◆ ◆ ◆

Desire was riding me hard, and the challenge of shattering Nicolas's ingrained control thrilled me. I ran my hands over him, fascinated with the width and length of his shaft, which was more than average. His skin was warm and smooth with distinctive strength encased beneath. I directed him to shift up so that I could slide the denim down his legs and then trailed kisses on the inside of his bronzed thigh. His muscles flexed there, and I found the sight fascinating. I let my lips drift to the other thigh in an attempt to elicit the same response. I slid my hands along his outer thighs, up his hips, to the planes of his abdomen, while I continued to rain kisses across his waist. It was a lazy exploration that had his hips straining off the couch as I seemed to ignore his stiff, burgeoning erection. When I finally gave in and grasped him in my palm, his sigh of relief was short- lived as I began to stroke him, and soon his hips were thrusting of their own accord once again.

I leaned down then, realizing that he was close to losing it. I needed to draw our encounter out a little longer. The desire running through me garnered a wickedness I never knew I possessed. Damien had dominated everything in our relationship, even sex, and had not once allowed me the freedom to explore my own willful desires. I pressed a kiss to the base of Nicolas's shaft, feeling his pulse there, and then ran my tongue up along the thick vein on the side to clasp his head between my lips. I could feel him shudder beneath me. His response caused yearning to coil within my abdomen, as moisture slickened my thighs.

I sucked his head—once, twice—before taking him deep within my mouth until the tip bumped the back of my throat. I applied just the right amount of suction as I allowed his cock to slide free, repeating the actions over and over again. I was clenching the walls of my sex as I rocked back and forth, sucking and sliding along his shaft until I felt his body tense. He was close to coming, his body straining. His hand came up to cradle the back of my head, sliding through the soft curls there as he guided me up and down his shaft, his breathing labored until he jerked and bucked, all the while my name a song upon his lips. He exploded then, hot seed filling my mouth. I drank every drop, sucking him as his thrust became jerky and uncoordinated.

I showed no mercy and was relentless in my pursuit. His member remained stiff with need as I continued to stroke him up and down, needing his salty taste to fill me again. His hands ran over my shoulders and cradled my head to him as he strained for release yet again. I alternated three short strokes with three deep ones, taking him as far into my mouth as possible, loving the feel of him, reveling in my power over such a masterful creature. Need tightened my womb, and I was hit with my own desire full force. Seeing his culmination as my own, I massaged his heavy sack, all the while continuing the relentless rhythm until I felt his muscles tighten beneath my touch again. He shouted my name in fulfillment, his salty essence once again filling me. Moments later, I was brought up short as Nicolas hauled me up into his lap so that I faced crystalline blue eyes that smoldered with passion. "Turnabout is fair play," he said, the wickedness of his smile promising seductive retribution.

Thirty-Two

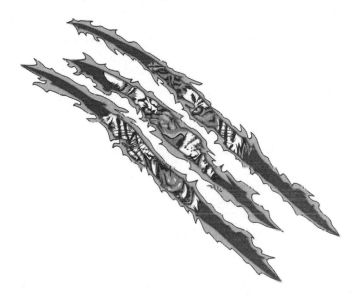

I stood up, grabbing Ieshelle so that she stood before me. I let my hands drift over her shoulders and down her back as I kissed the spot just above her collarbone. I slid my hands to cover her breasts, brushing my thumbs over the sensitive buds before drifting down her sides. Her breath was coming in short pants, and I was hard-pressed not to take her right here. My control reached new depths as I refrained from enacting that fantasy. Instead, I wished for our first time together to be completed in a bed. I continued my tactile exploration, moving my hands to cover her rounded derriere.

I lifted her in my arms and tossed her over my right shoulder. Unable to resist, I nipped the back part of her thigh just below the curve of her ass, only to ease the sting with a gentle kiss. *God, I love this woman!* My heart swelled at the thought. Ieshelle was not only beautiful but intelligent and caring. She had also given me the most intense pleasure, and now I had the freedom to bestow the same on her. This time was different, because I would claim her completely. On this night, there would be no stopping, no holding back. I would give her everything, and I expected everything in return.

"Where is your bedroom?" I asked as I moved toward the stairs. I nipped her again, which resulted in the most delicious squeal.

"Upstairs, to the left, last door on the right. You should see the light from the lamp I always leave on." Ieshelle sounded breathless, and that fact only heightened my need to see her shatter in ecstasy again. I found the room easily and was surprised to see that the bedroom was almost devoid of color—yet another contrast in her personality. The bed was a large chestnut sleigh with a white duvet and white pillows. The carpet was sandy brown, and the dresser, nightstands, and entertainment system were all chestnut. There were various brown pillows on the bed, and a white chaise lounge in the corner. This room lacked the vibrancy of all of the other rooms but spoke just as loudly of Ieshelle's character, even though it was devoid of color. The room was peaceful and calming. There were no butterflies here.

I stood her before the bed, running my hands over her ample curves until I reached her back. I let my hands continue around to cup her breasts, savoring their weight, flicking my thumbs over her distended nipples. Her hands wandered across my shoulders to cradle my face, her thumb tracing my lips with a whispered touch. I feathered my hand down her sides, pausing as my fingers encountered the faintly puckered flesh on her right hip. I bent to place a kiss there before continuing my descent. I clasped the waistband of her panties, sliding them down over her hips and thighs until they gathered at her feet. I lifted her again to lay her across the bed.

I left the light on, needing to see every inch of her, wanting to view every emotion that crossed her face when I claimed her. I stepped out of the denims and shorts to join her on the bed, taking my time to just look at her. Her breasts were perfect, lifted high, and overflowed my hands. The dark chocolate color of her nipples was a sharp contrast to the honeyed-almond color of her skin. I leaned down, taking a bud deep into my mouth, circling the other peak with my thumb. She began to moan and run her hands over my head, holding me to her. I slid my hand from her peak to cross her stomach and slide between the ebony curls that covered her womanhood. She jerked at the brush of my fingers against the swollen flesh, slick with her nectar. I moved over her, taking the abandoned peak within my teeth before sucking it deep within my mouth. All the while, I ran my fingers along the seam of her sex as her hips lifted and thrust in abandon.

"Nicolas . . ."

I knew what she wanted and as always, I could deny her nothing. I slid my finger within her folds, running over her swollen nub before sinking deep within her core. God, she was wet! I pumped my finger in and out as she began to ride my hand. Damn, she was so tight! I released her nipple, kissing up her neck to capture her lips. I caressed her sex, sliding my finger free. I needed to taste her; the memory of her essence called me. I flipped her over, covering her with my body, blanketing her with my warmth. I kissed the nape of her neck, running my hands over her arms as I moved down her back, placing kisses along her spine. Her breath was coming in small pants, and she moaned in frustration. When I reached the small of her back, I slid my hands around and guided her hips until she was raised up on her knees, my groin pressed against her backside. I slid one hand up to cup her breast while the other hand traveled once again between her legs to delve between her folds.

"Nicolas . . . please . . . I need . . . Nicolas!"

I moved her closer to the edge of the bed, keeping her on her hands and knees.

"Nicolas?" Ieshelle looked back at me, questioning apprehension in her eyes.

"Trust me, *ange*. I will not hurt you," I said as I placed a kiss against her rounded cheek and slid my finger within her core yet again. She closed her eyes, and I nipped her cheek, garnering her attention yet again. I needed her acquiescence before continuing. This was not an act to dominate but one to demonstrate trust. "Tell me, Ieshelle. Tell me what you want."

She took her bottom lip between her teeth before leaning back against me, causing my finger to slide deeper within her sex. "I want you to make love to me with your mouth."

Her request was my desire. I replaced my finger with my tongue, delving deep into her core before assaulting her tight bud. I massaged the sensitive flesh over and over again, using my fingers to open her to me completely. She dropped her shoulders, her head resting on the bed as her fingers grasped the sheets while she rode my tongue. The taste of her filled my mouth, and I could feel her straining for completion. I stroked her from clit to core over and over again, manipulating the sensitive nub on every caress until I felt her muscles convulse. I pressed my tongue against her clit as she exploded in my mouth.

I kissed up her back, bringing her bottom flush against my straining erection. The delicious friction caused by her slick folds coating me was nearly my undoing. I stretched out over her, blanketing her once again with my warmth yet sustaining my own weight. I intertwined our fingers as I kissed the side of her neck, thrusting forward as she rocked back against me. I kissed the sensitive spot beneath her ear, tracing the butterfly there with my tongue, before moving to the nape of her neck, between her shoulder blades—every place I had memorized that made her clench her teeth and catch her breath—all the while rocking against her clit, my hardened cock riding in between her slick folds as she pushed back against me. She came again, her body shuddering beneath me as she screamed my name, her flesh sensitive to the slightest movement.

"Nicolas, please . . . wait . . . please . . . don't move. Just . . . I need . . ."

"Shhh, love. Shhh!" I whispered as I gathered her to me. We lay on our sides so that my body cushioned her back. I just held her for a moment, letting the small shudders subside before I began round three. I watched and listened for the signs, waiting for her body to tell me she was ready. Her breathing had slowed, and she was once again grinding her hips against me, her body needy and in search of fulfillment. I kissed her shoulder as I cupped her breast, running my thumb over the stiff peak. "What do you want, Ieshelle? Tell me."

She took her bottom lip between her teeth again as she contemplated my question. "I want you to make love to me, Nicolas. I need to feel you inside me so much I ache," she confessed.

I kissed her neck once again before I rolled to my back, pulling her up so that she leaned over me. Her eyes searched my face questioningly, unsure of my intent. "Take what you want from me, Ieshelle," I said, offering the sweetest submission.

Thirty-Three

I looked into those compelling blue eyes, and the desire reflected there boosted my confidence once again. I straddled Nicolas, his hardened flesh flush against my sensitive core. I leaned forward, stretching out to cover him, taking his lips in a deep, seeking kiss while I rolled my hips. The friction created from his hardened shaft massaging against my sensitized flesh sent delectable waves through my entire body. Our eyes locked as I rose so that I hovered above him, his sex straining upward to meet me yet again. I grabbed his shaft, stroking the slickened hardness. I was fascinated once again by velvet-smooth skin stretched over muscled steel. I poised him at my entrance, never breaking eye contact, as I lowered my hips, taking him slowly into my body.

The first contact sent a delicious wave from my core throughout my entire being. Power flowed within me, as I was in complete control of the encounter, and I relished it. Seeking the pleasure I knew Nicolas offered willingly, I continued to slide along his shaft. Damn, he was big! I could feel the walls of my sex stretching to accommodate him, so far to the point that it was almost painful. The sensation of being filled was the greatest aphrodisiac, creating a fever within me. I needed more. I wanted Nicolas like no other. There was no one else, only Nicolas.

Need was too paltry a word for the emotion that filled me. I was rapidly being consumed by a frenzy of desire. I wanted Nicolas completely. I knew there could be some pain, but I wanted him so badly. It was madness. I tossed my head back in surrender, rocking against him as he slid deeper and deeper within my core. Panting, I squeezed my eyes shut from the pain and pleasure. Nicolas's hands upon my waist brought me up short, and I looked down to stare into his intense eyes. Sweat now covered his brow and chest, but a look of concern crossed his face, and I wondered again how he knew me so well.

"Go slow, Ieshelle. I'm not going anywhere." His voice was strained but a gentle command. He ran his hands up my hips to brush the underside of my breasts before continuing further until he cradled my cheeks. An involuntary shudder ran through me at his tender touch. I took my bottom lip in my teeth while he trailed his hands down again to fondle my breasts. I could feel myself slicken even more in response, allowing deeper penetration, as I continued to rock against him. I found an easy rhythm until I finally slid home, his manhood stretching and filling me completely. I paused a moment just to wallow in the joy and totality of being one with Nicolas.

I could feel him pulsing within me and could fight the temptation no longer. I began to move up and down, riding him with new found confidence, as he grasped my hips, his breathing erratic. I couldn't stop looking at him, glorying in his contained passion. I wanted to see him lose control completely again. I leaned back, resting my hands on his thighs as I brought my legs up for better leverage. The position allowed even deeper access, and I had to slow my pace slightly before increasing once again. Nicolas was now blowing like he had just finished a twelve-mile run. I couldn't help smiling, the vixen in me emerging even more as I squeezed my internal muscles and continued to stroke him. I had only completed the second thrust when he flipped me over, and I was staring up into his desire-filled blue eyes.

This was Nicolas, unrestrained. He held my hands in his, stretched above my head, and leaned down to rest his forehead against my shoulder. "Just give me a minute, Ieshelle. I'm sorry. I lost control for a moment."

I reached to stroke his cheek, clenching my muscles yet again. He groaned in response. "That was the point, Nicolas." I raised my legs up to his waist, giving him better access, as I slid my hands down his back. He groaned, a deep rumbling in his chest, before he leaned down and plundered my mouth with a branding kiss. He was lost then to his passion, which stoked my own to new heights. It wasn't long before I was clinging to him as an orgasm caused me to shatter in his arms. He continued to pump into me, his hips moving in sure and measured strokes.

"Nicolas!" I pleaded.

He understood what I asked for, and panting, he said, "I don't want to hurt you, Ieshelle. I can't!"

I ran my hand up his stomach, and the muscles contracted at my touch. I stopped just above his heart. "Get off me!" I commanded and gave him a hard shove.

"What the hell? Ieshelle?"

"Get off me, Nicolas!" I yelled again, beating at his chest. "If you can't be as open and free in this relationship as you want me to be, then we made a mistake! Get off!" I shoved again.

"Dammit, Ieshelle! Don't cry, baby. I'm sorry." Nicolas swiped at the tears that trailed down my cheeks. I hadn't even realized I was crying, but the fear that our relationship was going to end before it actually began made me realize just how much I loved Nicolas. We were walking a thin line—one wrong move either way and the whole thing could implode.

"Nicolas, I love you!" I confessed, unable to hold the words in any longer. "I'm not afraid to say that now. You have given me the confidence to admit it to you and to myself. I trust you, Nicolas. You have to trust yourself."

Nicolas leaned forward, understanding and resolve shining in his eyes. He placed chaste kisses on my cheek, my mouth, and my neck, his warm lips tempering the panic I felt. "I'm sorry, Ieshelle. Please, *mon ange,* stop crying," he whispered pleadingly. He continued to feather my lips and neck with kisses, as his hand came up to cup my breast. His touch was firm as he rapidly stoked my passion back to full arousal. The sobs were replaced with breathless, sighs of pleasure. He moved within me again, working me over until I was grasping his shoulders as wave after wave of pleasure descended over me.

Nicolas was adept. placing my legs over his forearms, the position opening me even further, like a blossom reaching for the sun.

He continued to move within me, each stroke placing him in direct contact with my sensitized flesh. His hips moved like a piston, and my dewy nectar coated him, allowing an effortless ride as he continued to stretch me within. I could feel him straining against me as my stomach tightened in preparation for release. Tiny webs of pleasure floated throughout my veins, building in intensity with each stroke, until my feeble body could no longer contain it. I splintered off into oblivion, as wave after wave of pleasure consumed me. I was brought back only by the realization that it wasn't over.

Nicolas slid my legs up to his shoulders, his hips continuing their assault as he pumped deep within my sex. Sweat slickened his skin, and small droplets fell on my face. His eyes were fierce, missing nothing as he sought completion, and I could deny him nothing. He leaned forward, grunting in his intensity as cum shot from the head of his sex, filling my womb. He spilled himself within me, his manhood still rigid with need.

The beast within him had been unleashed and continued to seek fulfillment. He flipped me over so that I was once again on my hands and knees, as he continued to move within my core. I arched my back, matching his rhythm in this position so that I was riding him once again. Nicolas held me to him, his hands on both sides of my hips, as he pounded into me, his balls slapping my core with each stroke. It was too much! Ecstasy flowed within me once again as I shattered over and over again. My essence, warm and slick, ran down my thighs, causing a loud, clapping suction as Nicolas continued to assuage his desire.

I screamed his name over and over again as I trembled in his arms. Multiple orgasms racked my body, finally causing him to spiral out of control. His seed filled me over and over until he was completely drained. He covered me once again with his warmth, his chest cushioning my back before we toppled on our sides. He groaned and then shifted to pull the sheet up to cover our sated bodies. We remained joined, his sex pulsing within my core, as he placed small kisses along my shoulder. His arm covered me as we fell into an exhausted sleep.

Thirty-Four

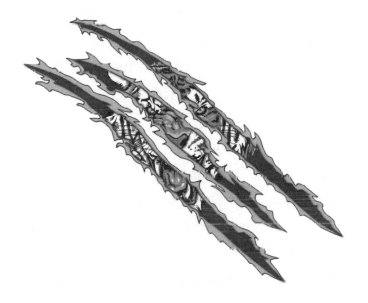

I sat up in bed, my back supported by the headboard, as I stared down at Ieshelle. She was sleeping, her dark lashes fanning her cheek. I had truly been an animal last night. It was as if I couldn't get enough of her. We made love three more times before the night ended and then once again just as the sun was beginning to shine through the window. I was insatiable. I loved this woman. I loved the way she bit her lip when she was contemplating things. I loved the way she laughed. I loved the way we fit together perfectly. I spent the remainder of the morning contemplating what to do about our relationship. In spite of Ieshelle's declaration of love, I felt that she would not believe a long-distance relationship could work. Everything was too new, still in its infancy, and we would have to test the foundation we had built through distance.

In spite of our being in a queen-sized bed, there seemed to be very little space. I felt like we were in a cocoon, with the scent of our loving surrounding us. Ieshelle snuggled closer, her arm tightening around me as she slept. I couldn't imagine waking up a day without her by my side. *How had these feelings grown so intense in such a short amount of time?* Sophie told me I had to be patient with Ieshelle, that she was stubborn. I had to trust that we would find our way through this. Ieshelle shifted, and I could tell she no longer slept.

"Mmmm! So, you are finally awake?" I asked as I pulled Ieshelle closer to me. I placed a kiss against her neck as I trailed my hand lazily from her breast to settle against her thigh.

"You've already been up?"

"Yes, sleeping beauty, I had to get up. My arm was feeling a little stiff, so I went through some conditioning exercises."

She sat up then, her exhaustion replaced with concern.

I smiled at the thought of all the positions and maneuvers I had used last night with her. I was sure she was remembering as well. "Ieshelle, I am fine. The arm is almost completely healed. I even told my manager to see about moving up the first fight."

"Nicolas, I don't think that is a good idea. You could reinjure it and make it worse if you don't let it heal properly," she reminded me.

I reversed our positions so that Ieshelle was on top of me, her legs straddling me lazily. "I need to get back in the ring, Ieshelle," I insisted. "You don't understand."

"Make me understand," she suggested as she stroked my cheek.

I turned into the caress, luxuriating in her touch, and placed a kiss in the palm of her hand. I looked up into those honey- colored eyes.

Ieshelle was my weakness. She was everything I had hoped to find in a woman. I wanted to share everything with her, even if it caused me great pain, embarrassment, and confusion. Emotions churned within me, and I knew I had focused on my desire and attraction to Ieshelle to avoid facing the fear . . . the regret . . . the anxiety. After losing my last match, my confidence was shattered. I had been undefeated up until that match and lost my title as a result. I played that fight over and over in my head, replaying the moves and recognizing the mistakes for what they were. I was known as "the Beast" because of my prowess in the ring. *How did I regain that confidence?* I slid Ieshelle from her position as I sat up, preparing to retreat. I needed time to work through everything.

I was caught off guard when Ieshelle shoved my shoulder hard, causing me to fall to my side. She leaned over me, her eyes blazing with anger. She had never exhibited this emotion before, and I was fascinated by the way her eyes seemed to glow, appearing more gold in color. She was magnificent! I reached for her, suddenly wanting her again with such intensity that I felt consumed by it. It was only when she swatted my hand away that I registered what she was saying.

"Nicolas, you don't get to do this to me! You don't get to make me feel . . . these . . . these emotions for you, make me admit these feelings, and then shut me out!" She was shaking with intensity, tears sliding unchecked down her cheeks. "You don't get to rescue me and set me free if I can't do the same in return!" I hadn't realized that was what I was doing, and I had no intention of hurting Ieshelle, ever! *Damn!* I reached up to wipe the tears from her cheeks, the moisture burning the tips of my fingers like acid. I hated to see her cry. This was twice now. *Shit!* My chest felt tight as emotions filled me.

"Ieshelle, I didn't mean to shut you out, it's just . . ."

She settled herself against me, pillowing her head on my chest as she laced our fingers. "Talk to me, Nicolas," she commanded, her voice tight with tears.

I kissed the top of her head as I tried to think of a way to make my confession. In the end, there was nothing to do but say it. "I'm scared, Ieshelle." There; I'd said it. I tried to stifle the anxiety that the confession made me feel, but it seemed to be swamping me. I had just admitted to my woman that I was weak . . . a failure.

"Relax, Nicolas. Talk to me," she prompted softly. Her easy acceptance caused me to relax and face my fear.

"I lost my last match due to submission. It's how my arm was injured—I was pinned with an armbar." I confessed.

"It wasn't the first time you lost a match, was it?" she questioned.

"No. When I was first starting out, I lost some preliminary bouts, but since launching my professional career, I had never lost a fight."

"What did you do after the last time you lost?" She snuggled against me like a contented cat, all the while calming my inner demon.

"I worked my ass off and came back and won the next match. I have won every match since then . . . that is until I was defeated."

"Even Lancelot fell off his horse. It was what he did afterward that proved his worth."

She was right. If you fall down, you get back up. My father had said something similar. I needed to push myself just as hard now, if not harder than the last time. I needed to go back to New Mexico. *But where did that leave us?* I pushed the thought from my mind as I rolled over, pinning Ieshelle beneath me. She let her legs fall open in accommodation, bringing my sex into intimate contact with her core. "So you think I'm a knight?" I asked.

She shook her head in denial as she lifted her hips, causing a delicious friction. I grabbed her then, plunging home, her sigh of content an echo of my own heart, before she caused me to lose all thought. Ieshelle raised up, pressing her supple peaks against my chest as she drew my bottom lip between her teeth. She licked the sting away before declaring, "No, you are definitely a *beast!*"

I lost my composure. All control was shattered by her words and actions as I moved within her, taking her with complete abandon yet again. Ieshelle enfolded me within her arms, matching each thrust, until she shattered, her walls milking me until I joined her in unbridled ecstasy.

Thirty-Five

Six weeks felt like six months. It was hard to believe I had known Nicolas so short a time. We spent every night together since the ball, mostly at my place but sometimes at his. He said he preferred my house; it was "homey," he called it.

My mother was transferred to the rehabilitation center and looked to be recovering nicely. We visited her every day, and her eyes seemed to light up when we entered the room. She had become especially fond of Nicolas. She was talking better now, and the speech therapist assured me that she was making progress.

Sheba, my mother's Rottweiler, was released from the vet and had acclimated herself to her new home with me. She was still indifferent to me, although she seemed to have bonded with Nicolas.

Nicolas was fascinating. We talked about everything, from politics to Picasso. He spent the majority of his day training or working with the acting coach and was resilient in his recovery.

When I got the latest report from his doctor stating that his test results revealed he would not need more additional therapy, I was dismayed. Today would be his last session. *What did that mean for us?* We hadn't talked about the future, other than his declaring that he wanted to be a permanent part in my life.

I looked at the report again before I got out of my car and headed in for Nicolas's final morning conditioning session. The front door was slightly ajar, which concerned me. As I walked in, I heard Nicolas arguing with someone out back.

"Nicolas, your arm is ready. You're ready. It's time we went back to New Mexico. You could have gone back a week ago, but you've been on cloud nine. You need to complete your training and get ready for the fight. Jacque has had the first fight rescheduled for two weeks now. You should be kicking your ass to get ready for Mark Hiden, making sure he doesn't kick your ass again, instead of playing house."

There was the sound of scuffling, and then Nicolas's voice—a menacing demand. "Don't ever refer to my relationship with Ieshelle again, do you hear me?"

"Dammit, Nicolas, don't you see she has you tied up in knots? You've been drawing this thing out with your arm to stay here in Las Vegas. I get it, Nicolas, I do. You're into her, but you can't have it all, not now. You have to choose."

"There is no choice, then. Ieshelle will always win."

Oh no! He can't mean what I think he does? Nicolas wasn't one to joke about such things, but he couldn't possibly give his career up for me! *What are we doing?* I sat my bag on the floor, my heart sinking, as thoughts swam in my head. My home was here; his home was . . . where? That depended on where he was training. *Were we deluding ourselves?* There was no way this could work! I stepped out onto the patio, prepared to face the music. The fairy tale was over, and reality was hitting us smack in the face!

Thirty-Six

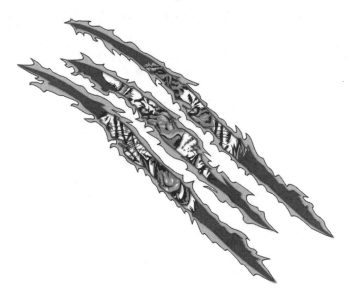

When I saw Ieshelle walk out onto the patio, her face spoke volumes. She'd evidently overheard my conversation with Frank and was ready to jump ship.

Dammit! I had hoped to have more time to talk to her before this issue came up. I signaled for Frank to give us a minute and walked back into the house, taking Ieshelle's hand in mine as I led her toward the stairs. She put up resistance once she realized where I was heading. I turned around to face her, tempering the panic that threatened to consume me. I had already thought about this and knew it would be strained, but it could work. There were two options: we could live between places, or Ieshelle could move to New Mexico. Since the latter was not likely, I would have to go with option one.

"Ieshelle, listen before you make up your mind about us," I pleaded.

She shook her head as she reached up to stroke my cheek. "Nicolas, you need to go to New Mexico, and I have to . . . I have to stay here. That's just the way it is."

"It doesn't have to be, Ieshelle," I pleaded. "Ieshelle, I need you!"

"Nicolas, I want this thing to work between us. I just don't see how it can right now. You need to train, and I am holding you back. Tell me the truth, Nicolas. Have you been delaying returning to New Mexico?"

"Not exactly. I—"

"Your big fight is coming up, and you yourself said that you needed to train your ass off if you are going to win your title back."

"Ieshelle, let me worry about that. It has nothing to do with us."

She turned then to storm away, only to stop and turn back around to face me.

"It has everything to do with us, Nicolas, and if you can't see that then it only reinforces what I know."

"And what exactly is that?" I challenged.

"Don't make me say it."

"Are you saying that you want to call it quits? You don't want to fight for our relationship? You don't want to try?"

"I didn't say that, Nicolas, but I'm trying to be reasonable."

"Dammit, Ieshelle, I love you, and you love me. You admitted it to me, and I won't let you take it back!"

"Nicolas, I do love you, but love is not everything in a relationship."

"So, what do you want? What do you expect me to do?"

"Go to New Mexico," she whispered.

"And what? Come by for a quick fuck whenever I'm in town?"

"No, I guess that wouldn't be a good idea, now would it?"

"Ieshelle—"

"Nicolas, just let it go." With that, she ran for the door, grabbing her bag on the way out.

I moved to go after her, but stopped short when I thought about what I was doing. Nothing I said to Ieshelle would help now. We were back to square one. Fuck! I just needed a little more time to get her to trust in me, in us. But no! The first little trial and she hightails it out of here. I threw the closest thing at hand—a vase of flowers—at the nearest wall; flowers that I had purchased for Ieshelle two days ago!

Frank stepped back into the house just as Ieshelle's car sped off. "So, what did you decide, Nicolas?"

"*I* didn't decide shit! I'm going to New Mexico, but when I come back, it will be not only to claim my title, but my woman!"

Thirty-Seven

I couldn't believe it had been three months since I cast Nicolas out of my life. Since then, I had gone through the motions the business was not providing the rewarding distraction I had hoped it would, in spite of being extremely busy.

Dr. Marcley had given a wonderful recommendation and the results of our therapeutic sessions with Nicolas were attributed to his rapid recovery. He completed his first match since the injury and was declared the winner by knockout. It bolstered my heart to know that he had achieved his goal and was one step closer to obtaining his title. I only wished I . . .I hadn't ruined things.

What the hell had I been thinking? The first major hurdle in our relationship, and I choked and ran away—or rather, sent him away. *Why had it taken me so long to figure this out?* I think it had a lot to do with the pregnancy scare.

My cycle was four weeks past due, and I was so sure that I was pregnant. The joy that filled me at the prospect of carrying Nicolas's baby helped me to realize how utterly stupid our argument was. In fact, I almost called him, but my cycle came two days later. The loss of that dream devastated me. I cried all day and night, so much so that my eyes were swollen the following day. I was confused, maybe it was a sign that we weren't meant to be together.

Nicolas called me every night, although I never picked up. I still couldn't face him, but I listened to every message, sometimes playing the recording over and over, just to hear his voice. I missed his accent. He continued to send me flowers once a week—it was his way of saying he had not given up on us and that the ball was in my court.

I didn't deserve him. I think that might be part of my problem—I felt like I didn't deserve to be loved by a man like Nicolas. I thought back to the last incident with Damien and realized I had been virtually running ever since, controlling all of my relationships and dropping those who had hope for a future. Nicolas was the only one I let past my barriers, the only one I'd brought into my home. But that still didn't solve the problem.

We loved each other—so what? Love doesn't make a relationship. Both of us were trying to complete goals we set for ourselves. Was there room for a long-distance relationship?

I dialed Eedie needing her advice, her familiar voice sounded through the receiver. "What's up Shelly?"

"Eden Rose?"

"Shelly are you okay? You sound like you are having a blonde moment, you did call me remember. What's up?"

"Eedie, how did you know Jacob was the one?"

"Hmmm, are you regretting your decision now?"

"Don't answer a question with a question."

"O-kay. Let's see . . . how to answer . . . If you really want to know, Shelly, I didn't know he was the one at first. Or maybe I did and I was too afraid to face it. I told you before we had a connection that I couldn't explain from that first night in the bar. I knew he was dangerous, but I couldn't stay away. We were drawn to each other. The next day he left a note, asking me to stay. He had an appointment he couldn't reschedule. I think Jacob knew then that something changed between us. I don't know how long I sat reading and rereading the note before I panicked. I left. I knew he wouldn't be able to find me. He didn't really know my name, but somehow fate put us back together again."

"I miss Nicolas," I confessed, unable to hold back the tears any longer.

"Is he still sending you flowers?"

"Yes." I sniffled as I dabbed at my eyes with some tissues.

"Is he still calling you every night and leaving you messages because you are too insane to answer the phone?"

"Yes."

"Then he misses you too. He also has not given up on you."

"I never said I didn't love him, Eedie, but why would I set myself up for hurt later when I know it can't work? We are moving in two different directions."

"Did you even try?"

"Well no, but that is only because—"

"You're scared of being hurt," Eden Rose interjected.

"Well, yes."

"One thing I have learned from Jacob is that men hurt too. Just like you, Nicolas is scared of being hurt, and every time you reject him, it adds to that hurt a little more."

I hadn't thought about how Nicolas was feeling; I had been so focused on myself and my demons. Nicolas had his own demons to contend with, and if Eden Rose was right, I hurt him every time I rejected him. I needed to think about what to do. I was still no closer to a solution, but I did have a better understanding. "Thank you, Eedie."

"No problem, Sis. How's your mom?"

"She's doing better. I just wish her recovery was faster."

"I'm glad she is doing so well."

"Thanks. How is your family?"

"Crazy as ever! This job with the track is more challenging than I thought, especially since I know just about everyone and their families. It's hard to talk to the families when you know them so well, especially if their loved one has been badly injured."

"Yeah, I guess that would be hard."

"Brian and Alexis make it better though. It's nice having my sister-in-law and her husband over, as well as their baby, BJ. He's like icing on the cake. He is so cute, Ieshelle. I have to send you the new pictures. I love playing auntie. I can't wait until Jacob and I are expecting our first."

I felt a familiar pang of jealousy at her happiness. She'd been afraid and had even run from Jacob, but he had not given up on her. Nicolas hadn't given up on me either, *but how much longer before that changed?* Eden Rose and I spent the next thirty minutes discussing plans for their visit here in six weeks. They would be here the same weekend of Nicolas's title bout because Jacob and Brian had a race at Las Vegas Motor Speedway the following day. As we chatted, I contemplated what to do about Nicolas.

◆ ◆ ◆

I held the cool steel in my hands, tracing the engraved initials DB on the handle as I watched Ieshelle get out of her car and enter the office building, her long legs accentuated by a slim white skirt. She wore a turquoise blazer with coordinated shirt and shoes, and her hair was longer than I remembered—well past her shoulders. She was beautiful, and my sex hardened at the sight of her delectable curves. I had missed her.

She had done well for herself, establishing her own business, a nice house, nice car, but she wouldn't have anything if it wasn't for me! I lost track of her after she escaped to Dallas and didn't expect her to move back to Las Vegas. She was brave! It was almost like a slap in the face for her to come back and establish herself like I never existed. Like Damien Brooks wasn't responsible for her success.

I had been watching her for the past few months with no sign of the monstrous boy-toy she had on her arm at the charity event. Maybe they broke up? *Perfect!* I wouldn't have to tussle with him again. He caught me by surprise that first time. I rubbed my jaw, remembering the sting of his punch. *Where the hell did she find him?* No matter. Ieshelle was mine and always would be. I was her first, and I would be her last! I tossed the hand piece into my glove box and drove off contemplating my options.

Thirty-Eight

I looked out of the terminal window at the mountains in the distance. Las Vegas. My heart beat in anticipation and fear. The last time I was here, I made a mess of things. I prayed that this time I would get it right. My fight was scheduled six weeks from today, along with a ton of publicity events to attend. My first instinct was to go to Ieshelle, drag her home with me, and convince her to give our relationship a chance, but I knew that wouldn't work. She still felt like our careers stood between us, and until I found a way around that, she would always come up with an excuse as to why it wouldn't work. Fuck! The shit was driving me crazy! Frank said that I had been acting like a wounded animal ever since we left Vegas, and I had to admit, I had been in a temper since leaving Ieshelle.

I pushed myself relentlessly during this training and initially lost twenty pounds but regained ten as muscle. I was in the best physical shape I had ever been in during my professional career. I ran miles and miles through the countryside trying to escape the visions of Ieshelle that assaulted me daily. I worked myself to exhaustion to escape the dreams of her that plagued me at night. It was torture. In addition to the fight training, I had completed my acting lessons and now spent time practicing my lines and fight scenes for the upcoming movie.

I would start shooting for the movie immediately following the fight which meant yet another separation. The movie was being filmed first in Miami and then on a private island in the Caribbean. I was really excited about the part even though it wasn't a starring role. I also liked that I got to be the "bad guy." It was a good role; the movie was about underground cage fighting. From the press and social media sites, it appeared my fans were ready for my acting debut.

I made sure to get one of the best coaches. I wanted to be believable. I wanted the viewers to leave the movie thinking, *Damn, Nicolas St. Pierre can act too.* I knew the movie would be good, *but what would Ieshelle think? Would she see my acting as yet another obstacle?* She'd had her heart broken; she was disillusioned and didn't trust her own judgment. How could I fight that? I hoped that if I were patient, she would see the error in her thinking, but it's been three months.

My cell phone rang, and Nicolette's face popped up on the digital screen.

"What?" I said as I picked up.

"Well, good afternoon to you too. How am I doing, you say? I couldn't be better. And you?" She sighed heavily. "That is typically how civilized people answer the phone, Nico."

"Good afternoon, Nicolette. How are you?" I asked, tempering my irritation.

"Fine, thank you. And you?"

Still in misery, I thought. "Nicolette, what can I do for you?"

"I . . . I just wanted to call to see how you are doing. I'm worried about you." She confessed. The sincerity clearly evident in her voice.

"I'll be fine."

"Will you? It's been three months, and you have been snapping at everyone, picking fights, and all-out brawling, according to Frank."

"You've been checking up on me?"

"Of course, I love you."

What could I say? "I'm doing my best. That's all I can do."

"Look, I know I was the one to tell you to be cautious, but seeing you like this really lets me know how much you care bout her. And according to Eden Rose, Ieshelle is no better."

"You talked to Eden Rose?"

"No, to Alexis but same difference. Ieshelle is just as miserable as you are. Only she is still too stubborn to admit it."

Stubborn. Her mother had stressed that Ieshelle could be stubborn. I looked down at my left wrist, noting the time. I had an hour, maybe two, before I was supposed to make my first appearance. "Nicolette, thanks for the advice," I said abruptly. "I will call you later."

I was going to see Ieshelle.

Thirty-Nine

I sat at my desk, attempting to work through the paperwork that was endless, but my mind kept drifting to Nicolas's last message. His title fight was coming up—I knew that, as the advertisements were all over the city. His message said he would arrive in the city today. I put my pen down and turned around to look out the window in my office. Typically, I would find peace in observing the view, but today none was forthcoming. What am I going to do?

After talking with Eden Rose, the thought of having Nicolas back in my life seemed promising, but none of my concerns had been resolved. If anything, they were more confirmed. Nicolas was here now, but after the fight he would be gone to shoot his movie. And then what?

My thoughts were interrupted as Lucy, a temporary assistant as Michelle was out on vacation, buzzed in that a gentleman was waiting to see me. "He says it's urgent and he's not leaving," she said.

I was just about to ask her to get his name when the door swung open unexpectedly. I tried to stop my heart from racing in anticipation of seeing Nicolas. I turned, expecting to see his bright blue eyes . . . and found myself staring at Damien.

"Damien, what the hell?" I snapped. "What are you doing here?"

He ignored my question as he closed the door behind him. He began walking around the room, running his fingers along the books on the shelves along the wall, all while stepping further into the room. I adjusted my vantage point, making sure that I kept the desk between us. I tried to still the panic that threatened to paralyze me. That would be a fatal mistake. I had to be alert. He was here for something, and somehow, I knew it would be painful. Keeping my voice as calm as I could, I said, "Damien, what do you want?"

Damien turned to face me then, his broad shoulders stretching against the confines of the obsidian-colored designer suit. "That answer has never changed, Ieshelle. I want you."

Although he was athletic in build, he was paltry when compared to Nicolas. He still wore the gold lion pinky ring on his left hand. I stepped back, remembering the way he used to make me kiss that ring to show my submission. I looked into his eyes then, and he smiled, flexing his hand, knowing what I had been thinking.

"You belong to me, Ieshelle. I gave you everything. It is because of *me* that you are the woman you are today."

"Damien, you need to leave before I call security."

He removed his jacket, folding the material slowly before placing it over the back of the nearest chair. He flexed his hands and then unbuttoned the cuffs of his shirt and rolled them up toward his elbow, as if he was preparing for a battle.

If he attacked me, there would be a battle; there always was. I was not meek—I never had been. I always fought back.

"Why do you always have to defy me, Ieshelle? I wanted this reconciliation to be civil, but as always, you want to force my hand." As he uttered those words, he advanced on me, and I screamed with alarm.

I tried to press the intercom for Lucy, but Damien attacked, knocking me down in the process. The back of my head struck the floor, the impact momentarily stunned me, robbing me of breath. As I struggled to sit up, he covered me with his powerful body, pinning me to the floor.

"Get off me!" I shouted in his face as I struggled against him. "Let me go, Damien!"

"Never! I thought I could let you go, but seeing you again has renewed my fire for you, Ieshelle. No other can take your place. Believe me baby, I tried. You belong to me and me alone!"

"I will never belong to you, Damien! Never! I'm not the stupid, gullible island girl you duped into loving you."

"Now, now, Ieshelle, you know it didn't take much to get you to come with me. I was even willing to bring your old hag of a mother, just to make you happy. But that wasn't enough, was it? No worry; since she is now in a nursing home, I won't have to worry about her poisoning you against me anymore."

"How did you know . . .? Damien, you're crazy! Get off me!" I shoved against him, but he grabbed both of my wrists, painfully jerking them above my head. As I tried to buck him off me, he pressed firmly into me, the ridge of his erection evident against my thigh, as the skirt I was wearing had ridden up during the attack. I shrank away from the contact as bile rose in my throat, nearly choking me. I prayed that Lucy heard my cry for help. I looked toward the door expectantly.

"Don't look for any help there, love," Damien snarled. "I sent your receptionist to grab us some lunch. She won't be back for a while. Just long enough for us to become *reacquainted.* Lucky us—everyone is out, so we are all alone."

I couldn't speak then, the hope for rescue gone. I was on my own. I lost it, knowing what he intended and not giving him anything. I couldn't stand him touching me. Bile rose in my throat again at the thought of him raping me in my own office. Tears welled in my eyes, but I blinked them back—there was no time for crying now. I had to escape.

Damien brought his mouth inches above my own, making me cringe. "Thoughts of tasting you again have given me many sleepless nights, Ieshelle. Lust that can't be abated, no matter how many women I take." His lips crushed mine in a brutal kiss.

Using my only recourse, I bit him, the taste of blood coppery on my tongue. Without warning, he released my hands, causing pins and needles in my fingers as circulation returned, I was so shocked that I was free, I didn't register his intent.

The blow to my left cheek swung my head to the right sharply, the impact causing blackness to swim before my eyes and my ears to ring. It was followed by two more blows that split my lip—the taste of blood in my mouth again was now my own. I could feel my lip and jaw swelling rapidly, and my head was pounding. It didn't matter. I would rather he kill me now than allow him to touch me again.

I went crazy then, biting and scratching at him—anything I could to get him off me. It seemed like my fighting only increased his lust, because soon he was tearing at my shirt and bra. I panicked as I felt the cool air against my chest. He tried to tear my skirt, but the garment was well constructed and wouldn't rip. Damien changed tactics. He ran his hand along my inner thigh to slide the skirt up to my waist.

I couldn't hold the tears back any longer—I would not be able to overpower him when I was so vulnerable. He pinned my wrists above my head again with one of his hands. My arms were battered and bruised from the struggle to the point of exhaustion. With his other hand, he pulled down the straps of my bra until my breasts fell free and lowered his head. I sobbed uncontrollably and writhed in protest as his mouth explored the swell of my breasts.

Suddenly, there was a loud crash, and Damien was wrenched from me. I immediately scrambled near my desk, attempting to grasp the remnants of my clothes to cover my nakedness. My head was throbbing so bad that the room swam before me, and every time I moved, my whole body ached from the abuse it had endured. My stomach was rolling, and I thought I was going to vomit at any moment. I heard scuffling and did my best to move toward the door—this was my only chance to escape. Suddenly, hands grabbed my shoulders from behind, and I went wild, thinking it was Damien again. The hands immediately released me, and I moved toward the door again, as tears filled my swollen eye and clouded my vision. I stopped scrambling only because I heard a voice that I would recognize anywhere: Nicolas.

I must have said his name aloud because seconds later, I could feel him next to me.

"It's me, Ieshelle. I won't hurt you, baby."

Nicolas was here! I collapsed against him, sobbing uncontrollably as his arms gently encircled me. He spoke softly in a mixture of English and French that calmed my distressed heart. "Damien . . ." I said tentatively, growing stiff with fear and panic, thinking that he could ambush us.

"Shhh, Ieshelle. It's okay. Frank and Jacque have him outside. The police and paramedics are on their way."

A blanket came from somewhere, and Nicolas wrapped it around my shoulders and then lifted me into his arms. I pressed closer to him, allowing his warmth to combat the chill and shakes that racked my body.

Nicolas is here. Everything will be all right.

Forty

I stood in the reception area of the emergency room, waiting for the medical staff to finish examining Ieshelle, and tried to calm the anger that threatened to consume me. When I thought about what would have happened to Ieshelle if I had not decided to see her before the first publicity event . . . I saw red. It had taken Frank and Jacque several attempts to pull me off Damien, and even so, he had several cuts and bruises, a broken nose and left orbit, dislocated shoulder, and a broken wrist.

It wasn't enough for what he had done to Ieshelle. The beast raged inside me, wanting more. I should have broken his jaw. I couldn't get the picture of Ieshelle out of my head— her sweet lips swollen from the assault, her beautiful face puffy and bruised from his abuse, as well as various other bruises on her body. I was still mad enough to kill! I think Frank realized that and stuck close to me. Jacque was on PR damage control and rescheduled the appearances that I missed today. I ran my hand over my head in frustration.

I kept pacing to expend some energy, as the need to destroy something still rode me hard. *Why the hell did he come after her now?* The more I thought about it, the more I realized that it had to be because of our last encounter, when he'd seen us together. He hadn't bothered her before. *Had I caused him to attack Ieshelle?* Shit! *But how did he know he could reach her? Had he been following her?*

My gut told me he had, and he probably realized that I was no longer there to protect her. *Shit! I had left her unprotected; it was my fault!* I slammed my fist into the nearest wall. The action eased some of the tension that filled me—so I did it again, the plaster crumbled under the assault. I was preparing for a third blow when Frank stepped toward me, and Jacque came at me from the other side. They both approached me as they would a wounded animal—cautiously. My rage had not dissipated; it still boiled under the surface, yearning for release.

"Nicolas?" She sounded like a frightened child, her voice soft and filled with tension, as if she was unsure if I was still there. I flexed the muscles in my hands, barely registering the sting in my knuckles as I turned to face her. Her face was not as swollen as it had been, but she was sitting huddled in a wheelchair, her shoulders covered with a blanket. Her shredded clothes had been exchanged for one of the generic blue-print hospital gowns.

I walked over to her and sat on my haunches so that our eyes were at the same level. "I'm here, Ieshelle." I grabbed her hand, and she noted the scrapes on the back of my knuckles, the skin broken and bleeding slightly after my encounter with the wall. She ran her fingers over my hands in a gentle caress, attempting to sooth the bruised tissue. How could she try to comfort me when she was the one who needed comfort?

"Nicolas, I want to go home now."

"Of course, *mon amour*," I said, ready to leave too. I signaled Jacque to take care of paying for the wall and any other damages or bills. The nurse handed me some prescriptions, along with discharge instructions, and explained what I needed to do while she wheeled Ieshelle toward the door. Frank had pulled the car around front and was waiting by the time we made it to the lobby. I helped Ieshelle get in the backseat and then joined her. Frank slid back in the driver's seat, and Jacque took shotgun. We rode in silence until we arrived at Ieshelle's house. I spoke to Jacque briefly before scooping Ieshelle from the backseat and taking her inside.

I secured the door and headed straight for her bedroom, where I sat her on the bed. She was so quiet—too quiet. I moved into the bathroom, starting the shower, and then looked through her dresser drawers to find her a comfortable nightgown. I pulled out a hot-pink sleeping shirt that had DIVAS written horizontally on one side in metallic silver, along with some white panties.

I placed towels and body-wash gel next to the shower for her, before returning to the bedroom. Ieshelle was lying on her side with her back to the door. She looked so small and frail, a sharp contrast to the strong, independent businesswoman I knew. I had to help her regain her confidence, just like she'd helped me regain mine. "Come on, baby, I have the shower ready for you."

She turned over then to face me, silent tears trailing down her bruised cheeks. I reached over to brush the wetness away, gathered her into my arms, and carried her into the bathroom.

I stood her before the cubicle and then pulled my shirt over my head, tossing it on the floor. "I'm going to help you with the shower, *ange*—that's all," I said.

The room had grown warm as thick steam billowed from the shower. I stepped out of the Timberland boots and removed the socks I was wearing. I unfastened my belt, letting the jeans I wore pool at my feet. I left my boxers on, so she would not misinterpret my intentions. As I stepped out of the jeans, a distinct blue pattern floated to the floor. I looked up to see Ieshelle standing before me, gloriously naked. I noted the bruises on her arms, hands, breast and thighs, where his finger imprints were now outlined by reddish-blue discolored tissue. I had to grit my teeth as renewed anger hit me. Ieshelle stepped closer, running her hands down my chest until they rested on my waist. She slid my boxers down to join my jeans on the floor.

She fell to her knees before me, her hands running up and down my thighs, as she blew her warm breath against my sex. I gave an involuntary jerk in response to her actions. I touched her cheek, causing her to meet my eyes, letting her know that she didn't have to do this—not now. The look in her eyes told me everything. Her control had been stolen, and this was her way of regaining some of that control. This was her choice.

I feathered my hand over her cheek again, and she turned into me, placing a kiss against my palm. She turned back and took my sex in her hands, her fingers sliding up and over the now-engorged head, causing me to groan.

Ieshelle moved leisurely, as if she was relishing each motion. The first touch of her lips against my sex caused me to jerk yet again in response, as she took me fully within her mouth. She continued her leisurely pace. Desire and need set a fire in my belly, and I was forced to lean forward against the shower door for support. I wasn't going to last; it had been too long since Ieshelle had touched me like this, since I had been alone with her. Visions of this very act had caused countless sleepless nights.

She switched the pace, going shallow, shallow, deep, as her hands fondled my thighs and burgeoning sac. Her teeth scraped gently along the fullness of my shaft, only to follow with another deep stroke that eased the sting, sending me over the edge as my seed filled her mouth in short bursts. Ieshelle milked me for every drop, her jaws holding me hostage as the orgasm raced through me.

She stood then, wrapping her arms around my waist before laying her head against my chest. I pressed my back against the wall as I fit her closer against me. I could tell she was crying, as her shoulders were shaking, and I lifted her in my arms to step into the shower. As the warm water washed over us, Ieshelle placed soft kisses against my neck. The multiple showerheads provided ample spray, and I leaned back on a wooden bench, allowing her legs to fall on either side of mine. I kissed her cheeks, her mouth, gently touching our lips and running my hands over her back as I held her to me.

Ieshelle opened to me, taking me deep within her core as she rode me completely unrestrained. I supported her weight with my hands, giving her the leverage she needed as she rested her hands against my shoulders. The water continued to cascade over us. I adjusted our position so that Ieshelle's back was against the wall as I moved within her. Her nails scored my skin, and I relished the sensation as I pushed deep into her core over and over again. Her walls contracted around me until she collapsed in my arms, her release draining the last of her remaining energy.

I washed us quickly before stepping out of the stall, noting that her eyes were drooping sleepily. I ran the towel briskly over her now-flushed skin, pulled the sleeping shirt over her head, and slid her arms through the sleeves. I dried her hair the best I could and then scooped her up in my arms to return to the bedroom, placing her under the warm covers.

I had just finished pulling on my jeans and shirt when the doorbell sounded. Ieshelle sat up in the bed alarmed, all signs of fatigue replaced by fear and apprehension.

"It's okay *ange.* It's just Frank and Jacque. They went to fill your scripts and pick up my car." I bent down to place a kiss against her forehead. "I'll be right back, Ieshelle, okay?"

"Okay, Nicolas." It was the first thing she had said since coming back from the hospital. Her voice was stronger and had lost the childlike quality it had taken after the attack. I was reassured by her tentative smile and knew she would be okay.

Frank and Jacque informed me that they would be back at eight in the morning to prep for the interviews that had been rescheduled, followed by training at my house. Jacque had silenced any reports related to Ieshelle's attack. They were also thoughtful enough to have stopped and picked up some sandwiches and drinks. As they were leaving, Frank hung back a little, looking as if something was bothering him.

"What's up Frank?" I asked.

"I'm sorry, Nicolas."

I stared at him questioningly. "What are you talking about?"

"Nick, if you had stayed like you wanted to, maybe thi . . . I mean . . ."

"Frank, it's not your fault. Damien is responsible for what happened today." *Amazing how easy it is for me to absolve Frank of guilt when I was thinking the exact same thing about myself earlier.* "I'm just glad we were there to stop him, or it could have been worse," I replied as looked toward the stairs.

"She's a special woman, Nick. Don't make the mistake of letting her get away from you again."

I closed the door behind him, knowing that I had to take my own advice and not blame myself for what had happened to Ieshelle, Damien was the cause of that. I placed the sandwiches in the fridge for later and grabbed a bottle of water and the pharmacy bag and headed upstairs.

Ieshelle lay on her side facing the door, her eyes wide, as if she had been waiting for me to come back. The tension seemed to drain from her limbs as I stepped into the room, and she relaxed against the pillows. I gave her the pain medicine and sleeping aid, removed my clothes, and climbed into the bed beside her. I pulled her close to me, blanketing her with my body, and she settled against me with a contented sigh.

Her head was pillowed on my chest as I ran my hand up and down her back, comfortingly, playing with the tendrils of her curling hair. I knew she had fallen asleep when her breathing came in smooth, even motions, but sleep eluded me. In my wakefulness, I contemplated how to convince Ieshelle to marry me, but I also formulated a plan to ensure that Damien Brooks never hurt her again.

Forty-One

It had been five days since the attack. I took off the rest of the week after the incident and intended to go to work on Monday after Nicolas left for the gym. But when Monday arrived, I pulled my clothes off and climbed back in bed. I just couldn't go back, not yet. On Tuesday, I was feeling better and worked from my home office, but I made an excuse to

Nicolas, saying that I was still tired and that I would go in tomorrow. I hadn't even been to see my mother. For some reason, I felt ashamed. Nicolas called throughout the day when he got a chance, and I did talk with my mother and Eden Rose on the phone, but I couldn't leave the house. It was Wednesday and I was still at home, and I had no intention of heading to the office. I was sitting at the table, sipping my second cup of coffee, when Nicolas strode in.

"I thought you were going into the office today," he said.

Nicolas was astute enough to notice I was avoiding the office.

Last night had been the first night since the incident that I didn't wake up screaming as Nicolas held me, and I sobbed until falling asleep again. I just couldn't go back to the scene of the crime. Two days after the incident, the police informed me that Damien had been released on bail. A police car was placed on surveillance outside the house for two days after that, but with no activity, they were later called off.

I didn't want to worry Nicolas, not when his fight was coming up in five weeks. He had been wonderful, staying with me every night since the attack, caring for me, and seeing to my needs. Nicolas helped me regain my sense of control, but I was still afraid. I thought I had closed the door to that chapter in my life, but Damien had come back and shaken my foundation—and I was terrified. Nicolas tried to hire a security detail, but I didn't want strange men following me around, and they sure as hell weren't coming into my house.

"Let's go for a ride," Nicolas suggested.

"What?" I was completely thrown with the change of subject. "Now?"

"You promised me a ride on your bike, and I am cashing in—today," Nicolas announced.

I knew there was a catch to this change in subject, but I was unsure of what it was. "Why today, Nicolas? What are you up to?"

"You can't stay cooped up in this house, Ieshelle. You have to go out eventually."

I knew he was right, but it was hard not to become defensive.

"Nicolas, I'm not staying cooped up."

"That's bullshit, and you know it, Ieshelle. You are hiding out in this house! You can't let Damien win—and he does win if you cower here, afraid to live outside these walls. Damien is not going to hurt you ever again. Trust me to take care of you! Don't let him make you afraid. Don't let him have that power over you." Nicolas was right—I couldn't let Damien win.

"Okay, Nicolas," I said with resolve, although that didn't lessen my anxiety. I went upstairs to change into black fitted jeans, a black muscle T-shirt, and biker boots. I grabbed my helmet and headed toward the garage. I could feel Nicolas at my back and was comforted by his presence. I'd bought this bike with my first big payday after I graduated from university.

It was a 2007 Ducati 1098. I had it detailed and stripped of its original paint. It now sported the colors of the Jamaican flag, with the gold saltire on a green and black field design over the tank. I remembered why I'd chosen the flag—not only because it represented my nationality, but because of what the flag symbolized. The color black represented the strength and creativity of my people, which allowed us to overcome all odds. Gold was for the sun that shone like a diamond over the island, and green was for the lush vegetation that nourished the inhabitants. I felt empowered the first time I rode the bike.

The wind in my hair and the power between my legs—it was exhilarating. I hit the button to raise the garage door, and I suddenly was anxious about starting the ride.

I cranked up the bike and beckoned to Nicolas to get on behind me. I gave him the extra helmet that was hooked to the back, and we were off. His hands circled my waist, and his strength and that of the bike melted the fear and anxiety that had chilled me from within. We rode for a while, the wind in my face, as the bike moved swiftly over the terrain. I didn't know where we were going until we pulled up to my office building, and I parked the bike in my usual spot. It wasn't the first time I had ridden the bike to work, so the staff was not surprised with my attire. They were extremely happy to see me back, I noticed as I made it to my office amidst hugs from various personnel. I held the tears in until we reached my suite, and Nicolas pulled me into his arms.

"They love you too, Ieshelle. They were just as worried about you as the rest of us."

I slid my arms around his waist and pressed my head against his chest, soaking up the comfort and support he offered. It wasn't until

I looked around that the fear returned and the attack started playing over again in my head. The office had been cleaned; the broken glass and papers no longer littered the floor. But I couldn't see that. All I saw were the images of that night. I started backing toward the door, but Nicolas grabbed me and held me to him.

"Ieshelle, calm down. I understand. You see the attack, don't you? Every time you look around, you are reminded of what happened here, yes?"

I nodded my head and closed my eyes to block out the sight of the familiar room. That only made it worse, as the images danced across my eyelids. I opened my eyes, blinking quickly to dispel the memory when I noticed that Nicolas had removed his shirt and was in the process of taking off his Timberlands. "What are you doing?" I croaked.

"Making new memories." He pulled me into his arms, covering my mouth with his own. I melted against him; his passion was infectious, quickly wiping away thoughts of the past. I could only think of him, and how much I wanted him inside me. Soon, I was making distinct keening noises in the back of my throat, needing more—needing Nicolas to the point that I was frantic. My hands were uncoordinated as I unfastened his pants, pushing them down toward his thighs. He grabbed my hands, lifted my shirt over my head, and tossed it behind him, before steadfastly undoing my pants, pushing them, along with my panties, down to my ankles. He unfastened my bra and lifted me into his arms, taking my mouth in a heated kiss. He consumed me. I could think of nothing else but him and the need that raged between us. I needed him inside me, filling me, staking his claim for all time.

There would be no time for preliminaries this go around, no time for foreplay. Nicolas cleared the desk with one sweep of his hand, and moments later, the cool wood was at my back. I opened to him instinctively, and he claimed me in one swift thrust, sliding home, my body more than ready for his infiltration. I realized then that I was not the only one that was fighting memories of the attack. Nicolas needed this coupling just as much as I did. I wrapped my legs around his waist, urging him into action. His hips moved in a piston motion, and I gripped his shoulders to sustain the ride.

It would not be long. I could feel my stomach contracting as the orgasm gathered within. My muscles bunched until darkness flashed before me, and I tipped over into delirious oblivion. I knew Nicolas had joined me, as my name was the last thing I heard on his lips.

Forty-Two

I had just exited the ring, the sparring match complete. I was ready to go home, even though I wouldn't be going to my house. I now understood the phrase, 'Home is where the heart is.' My heart was with Ieshelle. I still couldn't believe it. I also didn't trust it. Things were going well, but it was only because of the attack. She was still recovering. Somehow, I knew this bliss was only temporary. We didn't talk about the future. I didn't broach the subject, because I wasn't ready to give her up yet. I still hoped that by my being with her every day, supporting and caring for her, she would finally believe in our love.

I took the towel Frank offered, wiping my face before removing the sparring gloves. My arm was at full strength, and I was ready for Mark Hiden. I was confident that I would reclaim my title. I only wished I was as confident about the battle I waged to win Ieshelle's heart.

I shook my head as I headed toward the house, Frank trailing behind me. "Nicolas," he called out, "I want to ask you something."

"What's up?"

"I thought about what you said—that Damien must have been following Ieshelle. I know you've been picking her up from work, making sure she is never alone, but what happens when we leave?"

I grit my teeth, trying to prevent myself from growling at him. I didn't want to think about leaving Ieshelle again.

"I tried to get her an expensive security detail, but she vetoed that idea real quick!"

"Hear me out, Nicolas. She still doesn't feel safe, and you don't feel comfortable leaving her alone. So, what if you didn't have to?"

"What are you talking about, Frank?"

In response, he stopped and waved to Anthony Lawson, a familiar face, although one I hadn't seen in a while, beckoning him to join us.

"Hey, Nicolas, Frank tells me you might need my services."

Then it clicked for me. "Tony, I think he is right," I said. "You own a private security agency now, don't you?

"Yeah. Couldn't be a military man forever."

The wheels in my head started turning as I contemplated everything. Maybe instead of an entire security detail I needed just one man...a one-man army. I directed Tony into Frank's office so I could give him the intel on Ieshelle's case. I could hire Tony to be Ieshelle's protection while I was not around. He was trained for these types of missions and Ieshelle wouldn't even know that he was there. She would be safe. He also could do some field work and find out everything there was to know about Damien Brooks.

❖ ❖ ❖

An hour later, Tony was on his way to gather information on Damien, and I felt lighter on my feet, as if a great weight had been lifted. Ieshelle would be safe; Tony would take care of her. We worked out the payment details, and I paid the first installment so that Tony could begin immediately. With that problem solved, it still left the trust issue with Ieshelle.

I didn't know how to help Ieshelle feel more secure, to trust me completely, and most important, to believe in us. Her faith in relationships was so fragile . . . I didn't know what to do. I've been visiting Sophie with Ieshelle every day, and when I was away, the phone calls I made to Sophie helped sustain me. Sophie reminded me of her warning—that Ieshelle was stubborn and that I would need enough patience for us both, but damn! I didn't think I could stomach her rejection again. She was not the only one whose feelings were involved.

The fact that Ieshelle didn't answer one phone call while I was in New Mexico was distressing. I would have loved to have heard her voice just one time, even if it was to yell at me to stop calling. That's how I figured out she was listening to the messages. She didn't call me and demand that I stop harassing her. She also didn't block my number. That gave me a glimmer of hope that she still cared, but she was just afraid of being hurt again. I thought about what Nicolette said, maybe I was more vulnerable than I first believed. I just pray that I am not delusional, being willing to believe the smallest thing is a sign of Ieshelle's affection. *Damn I got it bad!*

Forty-Three

I sat at my desk, unable to see anything but the memories that Nicolas and I created within the confines of my office. The nightmare of Damien's attack was banished completely from my thoughts. Everywhere I looked in my office, I was reminded of Nicolas—his touch, his kiss, his passion. Nicolas had an insatiable appetite and knew how to elicit the wanton vixen within me. I had a delicious ache between my thighs that was a constant reminder of his virility and had me smiling and blushing continuously throughout the day.

Three weeks remained before Nicolas's fight, and then he would be off to Miami to shoot the movie. I still had not decided what could be done for our relationship. I was a realist and was not optimistic that a long distance relationship would work. I knew Nicolas loved me, but love did not make a relationship. People hurt the ones they loved all the time, whether intentionally or unintentionally. I just didn't know what to do. The sound of the phone ringing interrupted my deliberations.

"Shelly?"

"Eedie? I thought you had lost my number or something," I teased.

"No, just been busy with the hubby and the new job."

"How is Jacob?" I asked.

"Scrumptious as ever! In fact, he was just pictured on the cover of *GENTS* magazine."

"Was he, now? Congrats! So, when will I get to see you, Eedie? I feel like it's been ages."

"It's only been a couple of months, hon. Still undecided on what to do about Nicolas? I hate that he wasn't there the last time I was in town. I would have loved to meet my future brother-in-law."

"Eedie!"

"Mark my words."

"Eedie, be serious."

"I am."

"I don't know what to do about him."

"What do you mean, Ieshelle? He's supported you through this whole ordeal with Damien. He said he loves you, and I know you love him, so what's the holdup?"

"His main training facility is in New Mexico, Eedie."

"And? I thought we already covered this," she chided.

"Right now, my life is here in Las Vegas," I reminded her.

"I don't know what to say, Ieshelle. I know you're referring to your mom when you say your life is in Vegas, but somehow it will all work out, you'll see."

"Eden Rose, he said he wants to be a permanent part in my life. I still don't know what that means."

"Have you asked him?

"Well, no," I responded as I doodled Nicolas's name at the edge of the legal pad on my desk.

"What do *you* want, Ieshelle?"

"I know what I *don't* want; I don't want to be hurt. I'm afraid."

"I know, Ieshelle. It can be scary to trust someone so completely, but look at the alternative—being alone. None of us want that. You have to stop being scared and take chances. I want you to be happy. As far as I can see, you've never been as happy as you are with Nicolas. You have to take a chance."

I knew in my heart she was right, but it was hard to get my head to agree. Before I could respond, she abruptly changed the subject.

"Look, Shelly, I almost forgot why I called. We will be in town in three weeks. I wanted to know if we are still on for the fight. That way I could scope out Nicolas and tell you what I think."

"Yeah, yeah, sure, sounds good." *Maybe I will have decided what to do by then*, I thought.

"Talk to you in a couple days, Sis; I promise." Eden Rose replied before hanging up the phone. I hung up and contemplated everything Eden Rose had said. It was along the lines of what I had been thinking already, *so why was I still so confused?*

The phone rang, and I thought it was Eedie calling me back, but the crisp voice on the phone caused my chest to tighten.

"Ieshelle Jones?" I remembered the last time I'd received a phone call like this; it had not been good news.

"Yes, this is Ieshelle Jones."

"Ms. Jones, this is Alice Rector from Sunnydale Nursing and Rehabilitation Center. I'm calling because we had to rush your mother to the hospital today."

Suddenly, I couldn't breathe, "What do you mean? What's going on?"

"She was taking a nap—she complained of a headache earlier, and—"

"What happened?"

"I couldn't wake her up. That's when we rushed her to the hospital. The doctors think she might have had a stroke." When I didn't respond, the nurse attempted to gain my attention.

"Ms. Jones? Ms. Jones? Are you there?"

I dropped the phone without responding and grabbed my purse as I ran out the door. *I can't believe it. She was doing so well.* The doctor had even mentioned that she might be able to come home soon. Tears burned my eyes as I got in the car.

Forty-Four

I tried to call Ieshelle again. It was the fifth time tonight with no answer. Where the hell was she? Fearing that something was wrong, I called Tony. I paced as I waited for an answer. If Damien . . . Fuck! If Damien has touched her again, I will kill him!

"Lawson."

"Where the hell is she?" I questioned, without preamble.

"She just pulled up outside of Cedars Hospital. I was just about to call you myself. She looks as if she has been crying, Nico."

Why the hell would she be at the hospital? Sophie! "Shit! I know why she's there. I'm on my way. Don't let her out of your sight!"

"Already on it, Nico."

◆ ◆ ◆

I found Ieshelle sitting in the chair next to Sophie's bed in the emergency room. I looked at Sophie in disbelief that this was the same woman I had visited just yesterday. She was hooked up to a ventilator and was so pale. I looked at Ieshelle, and her face said it all. It was worse this time.

I stepped up to the bed, and Ieshelle fell into my arms, holding on to me for dear life. Sophie was too young to have a ruptured brain aneurysm and a stroke—she was only fifty-two.

Just as Ieshelle's breathing seemed to calm, the door to the room opened, and a solemn-looking Asian man entered. He was wearing sea-foam green scrubs and a white lab coat that had seen better days. Ieshelle turned in my arms, but I held on to her, as I determined by the doctor's expression that the news was not good.

"Ms. Jones, your mother's MRI results are in, and I am sorry to tell you that they are not good. There has been significant brain damage. She was placed on the ventilator after she coded again when she arrived to the ER. She is currently stable, but I'm ordering an EEG to determine if she has any brain activity. We will move her to the ICU until the results of the scan are in."

Ieshelle's legs buckled, and I caught her to me as her pain- filled sobs filled the air. I nodded to the doctor, and he slipped out. I whispered softly to Ieshelle, trying to comfort her, all the while my own heart was breaking.

◆ ◆ ◆

I carried Ieshelle into the house and upstairs to her bed. She was exhausted. They had moved her mother to the ICU. Damn! I had grown fond of Sophie and enjoyed our talks. If it wasn't for her, I would have given up on Ieshelle a long time ago. Sophie told me Ieshelle was a fighter, and although that was a good trait, sometimes it interfered with her decisions, especially when the person she was fighting was herself. Sophie believed that Ieshelle felt she didn't deserve to have me in her life. As crazy as that sounded, I knew that was what was holding her back. Damien had hurt her, physically, but the mental damage he caused still lingered. That was harder to combat than his physical abuse. I couldn't fight the past. I could only try to make new memories that would banish the bad ones.

I thought we'd been making progress after the incident with Damien but now there was yet another tragedy in her life. If she was true to her pattern, she would retreat. Damn! I tried to follow Sophie's advice to be patient, but damn!

I walked downstairs and let Sheba in so she could eat. I then looked through the fridge for something for us to eat later. I settled for soup and sandwiches. I went outside and played with Sheba, needing to expend some energy. The massive pup was begging for my attention.

When I returned to the kitchen, Ieshelle was at the stove, heating the soup and making the sandwiches. She put them in a Panini press and then made two salads. Her motions were stiff and sure, evidence of the strain that she was currently under. She should have been resting, but she clearly needed to control something in her life, even if it was as simple as preparing a meal. I sat at the table and watched her quietly until she came over and placed the plate in front of me.

We ate in silence until our plates were clear and Sheba was jumping on the back door to come in. She was a great dog and had really taken to me since the first day I met her, though she was impartial to Ieshelle.

"You shouldn't indulge her," Ieshelle said. "She was pining for days after you left the last time."

"What are you implying, Ieshelle?"

"Nothing, only stating the truth. Your fight will be over soon, and you will head back to New Mexico, or is it Miami? You shouldn't pay her so much attention. She will get attached again, only to have her heart broken."

"Are we talking about Sheba, or are we talking about you?"

"Nicolas . . ."

"I wasn't the one who gave up on us," I snapped. "And I'm not the one who is giving up on us now!"

Suddenly, I needed some air. I knew what she was doing, but that didn't stop the pain of her rejection. I took a deep breath and said softly, "Ieshelle, you're scared to be alone, yet you're too scared to let me love you. You have to decide what you want to do. I love you, and I know you love me, but you have to make up your mind to trust in us. Only you can decide that." I pulled her to her feet to kiss her on her cheek. "I'll be back tomorrow. Call me if you need anything."

I walked out of the house, hoping I hadn't made a mistake in taking a stand. I could lose her forever. *Or was I deluding myself? Maybe I never had her at all.*

Forty-Five

W hat had I done? Nicolas was gone again, when I wanted desperately for him to be here with me. I let Sheba in the house, needing what measly comfort she would offer me. *Why was I pushing him away when what I really wanted was to hold him to me? What have I done?* I am going to be all alone. Thoughts of my mother . . . my mother . . .

Tears flowed freely down my cheeks. It was amazing how things could change in twenty-four hours. Yesterday, Nicolas and I had eaten dinner in this room after visiting my mother. She had looked so much better and appeared to be recovering. *Why had this happened to her?* I could still hear her voice, chastising me for being so stubborn where Nicolas was concerned.

I sobbed, swiping at the tears that wouldn't stop falling. *I need Nicolas. Oh God, I need him!* I sat on the couch in the living room, staring out the window at the night until sunlight chased the darkness away. I didn't know what the day would bring, but I'd been too afraid to close my eyes and sleep.

◆ ◆ ◆

Three days later I sat at the funeral home on the pew surrounded by my friends and coworkers. And then there was Nicolas. I had only talked to Nicolas briefly in the days since the incident in my kitchen. My mother had coded again that night, and her body was unable to recover. I had to let her go. Nicolas was there to support me.

The memorial service was small and short but still beautiful. My mother looked so peaceful—rested. The lines on her face smoothed, the pain gone. She would be cremated, and I would take her ashes back to Jamaica. *And then what? What would I do then?*

Nicolas stood silently waiting for me. He had been very solemn during the ceremony, and I noted tears in his eyes as he brushed my mother's cheek for a last caress. His mother and father had come for the service, along with Nicolette.

The nurses at the nursing home had been saddened to hear about my mother's passing. They said that she had shown improvement, especially after her son had started calling three months ago. They thought she would be going home. Nicolas. He had called her every night, just like he called me when he was in New Mexico.

Too much was happening too fast. I felt like I was spinning out of control. "Nicolas, I'm ready," I whispered. He took my hands in his and helped me up from the pew. I was wearing a brightly colored floral sundress that was my mother's favorite. I had asked that everyone refrain from wearing black and somber tones and instead opt for the bright colors that reflected my mother's personality. Nicolas wore a steel-blue suit with a sunflower-colored dress shirt and coordinating tie. The colors complemented Nicolas's bronzed skin and accentuated his remarkable eyes. Yellow had been my mother's favorite color, and I was sure Nicolas had made the choice for that reason.

We pulled up to my house, and I got out of the car. Nicolas stood before me, and I wanted to pull him to me, but I needed . . . I . . . was so confused, and he just confused me more. I looked up into those clear blue eyes that could singe me with passion, eyes that were looking at me in concern and uncertainty. I had done this to him. I stepped up to circle my arms around his waist, placing a kiss on his cheek before I turned toward the house.

"Ieshelle . . ." His voice was tight with emotion. I turned, only to be pulled to him as his lips descended upon mine. The kiss was feverish, filled with the passion that boiled within him, even as uncertainty and anxiety stood between us. I drank him in, and the coldness that had descended melted slightly until I pulled back, knowing I had to let him go, I couldn't keep taking and taking from him with no hope of loving him as he deserved to be loved.

"Good-bye, Nicolas," I whispered before hurrying into the house and closing the door.

I collapsed in a fit of tears as I heard him slam the car door and speed off. It was done. I had set him free.

Forty-Six

I drove around for hours before finally heading back home. Only I wasn't home; I wasn't with Ieshelle. Damn. I knew what she was doing, but it didn't make the pain I felt from her constant rejection any easier to handle. I had done everything I could to support her and show that I loved her. I thought actions were louder than words, but maybe that wasn't enough for Ieshelle. I sat in my car in front of the house, contemplating my options. Nicolette opened the front door, I got out of the car, even though I wasn't in the mood to talk.

"Hmmm," she said, appraising me. "I can only guess that something happened between you and Ieshelle, seeing as how you are here and not there."

"Nicolette, I really am not in the mood right now."

"Nicolas, try to remember that a lot has happened. She might just need some time."

"Damn, Nicolette. What about me? Don't you think this shit has bothered me too? I cared about Sophie too! I just thought we. . ." I ran my hand over my head and then pinched the bridge of my nose as my eyes began to sting. *Ieshelle had said goodbye—not 'see you later' or 'I'll call you tomorrow,' but goodbye.*

"You thought you would share the pain together," Nicolette suggested.

"Yeah. I did." I took a deep breath. "I thought we could be there for each other." I moved into the house, pulling the tie from my neck and tossing it on the couch. Nicolette followed, closing the door behind her.

"Nicolas, Ieshelle is an independent woman—a woman who's been hurt in the past and had to fight to regain that independence. It's hard giving that up, letting yourself trust and rely on someone else." Nicolette walked past me toward the bar to pour two snifters of brandy. She turned around, offering one of the glasses.

"She told me good-bye," I stated simply before downing the drink and walking past Nicolette to refill the glass.

Nicolette didn't seem surprised by Ieshelle's actions. "Yeah, but did she mean it, Nico? She might have believed she was doing the best thing. Maybe she thinks she's not being fair to you because her feelings for you are not completely clear."

"How do you know this?"

Nicolette shrugged. "If I were in Ieshelle's shoes, I would be feeling very confused and overwhelmed. She might just need some time to think. You know—to clear her head. Don't give up on her yet."

"You sound like her mother now. Sophie told me that all the time—that Ieshelle was stubborn and I had to have patience with her."

"Well, then that should tell you something. I know what I am talking about." Nicolette plopped down on the couch, propping her feet up on the ottoman.

"What do you think I have been practicing for these past four months?" I asked as I sat down next to her, taking another sip of the fiery liquid.

"Yes, while you were in New Mexico, but what did you do when you got back? In light of the circumstances, Nicolas, I completely understand what happened but—"

"I pounced. I had every intention of taking things slow, but there was the attack with Damien and—"

"And wasn't it the first incident with Damien that made you speed up your relationship with Ieshelle initially?" Nicolette asked as she swirled the brandy around in her glass.

"Yeah, but—"

"Then it seems to me, Nico, that you need a new definition of patience."

I leaned my head back against the cushions as I realized I had made yet another fuck-up with Ieshelle. "Yeah, maybe you're right, but it doesn't stop the shit from hurting!" *No matter who is to blame.*

"I think it's because women forget that men can be just as hurt and wounded as women, even though most men don't show it."

I looked up as my mother entered the room, holding a stack of laundry. I sat the glass on the table, rushing over to help her. She probably had cleaned the whole house this afternoon. I looked at Nicolette questioningly, and she shrugged her shoulders, a mischievous smirk on her lips as she snuck off to her room. My mother gave me the same speech as Nicolette, only this time the French version.

Forty-Seven

I looked out at the greenery and tropical flowers that filled the yard of our Jamaican home. I had been here only three days, and I felt closer to my mother now. A quiet peace had settled in my heart, and I was able to accept her loss.

What I hadn't been able to accept was the loss of Nicolas. He haunted my dreams and complicated my days. He was always on my mind, only this time, he didn't call or send flowers; he wasn't there. I cried endless times and was at a loss about what to do. I knew I was the cause of my current predicament, but I didn't know how to resolve it. I still didn't have any answers about our future.

I looked at the tree in the backyard that my mother had planted when I was born. It was my escape when I was little, a place of mystery and dreams. My mother and I had spent endless hours, talking and reading to each other as we lay under that tree. It was where Antonio and I played hide-and-seek and where I first learned to paint and completed the portrait of my mother that now hung in my house. I buried her ashes at the base of the tree and mixed them in the fertile soil, so that she would forever be with her beloved Jamaica.

I walked back into the house and laid on the couch, staring up at the ceiling fan, a pastime to which I had grown accustomed since returning to my native land. Thoughts of Nicolas and everything I faced in Las Vegas would drift through my mind, often until I fell asleep.

I was staring at the canopy of leaves overhead as my mother read softly to me about lands far away and princes with vigor and charm. Her hands drifted through my hair, which was slightly curly and disheveled from the wind. My head was in her lap. I was only half listening to her as I watched the butterflies dance through the sky overhead. I loved butterflies—their colors, their mysterious beauty. Suddenly, the sky filled with dark clouds, and the heavens opened up to flood the land with Mother Nature's tears.

I woke up with a start as thunder reverberated throughout the house. I had fallen asleep. I sat up and ran my hands over my face. From the couch I could see the kitchen table and noticed that the black sealed envelope I had brought with me from Las Vegas was there. The envelope had been found amongst my mother's things at the nursing home, but I was sure I'd left it in the bedroom. I walked over to the table, stared at the envelope a moment, and decided that it was a sign that I should open it.

Inside was a letter penned in unfamiliar handwriting, even though it was a letter to me from my mother. I collapsed into the nearest chair, unable to sustain my weight as I stared at my mother's message from beyond the grave.

Dearest Ieshelle,

If you are reading this, then I am no longer in this world and have passed on to the hereafter. I am secure in knowing that you are not alone, for you have found Nicolas.

He is a strong man with a gentle heart, and I know he will make a great husband and father.

It is my fault that you are so afraid of the love he is offering you. I did this to you. I often thought that I was the cause of your choosing Damien too. You were so young and insecure and . . . lonely after Antonio's death. In spite of the love and attention I gave you, you still needed your father, and the loss of Antonio only seemed to cause you to become more insecure and depressed. I see that now, and I only pray that I am not too late in telling you this before you push Nicolas away forever.

I never talked about your father because I was too embarrassed about what I had done. I made the mistake of pushing him away and believing that I did not deserve the type of love he offered me. I believed that I wasn't worth it and wasn't good enough for him. When I realized that I was wrong and that I wanted his love, it was too late—he had married and started a family of his own. I had missed my chance.

I never told him about you, and I'm sorry that I'm telling you this now, amid the other pain and loss you must be feeling. I was too ashamed and embarrassed, and there was his family to consider. What right did I have to complicate his life? He didn't deserve that. All he had ever wanted to do was love me, but I was too afraid to let him.

You often asked me why I never talked about Antonio. I never answered because I didn't know what to say. I loved your brother with all my heart, but I was not in love with his father. I knew I would never love Johnathan because my heart was forever lost to another man. Johnathan was even willing to marry me in spite of knowing this, but I just couldn't see myself living a lie. I already had enough to answer for. I never wanted to talk about Antonio because I was ashamed that I had a baby by a man that I didn't love. But I was so lonely, and just needed...

Ieshelle, I recognize now how I robbed you and Barnibus, and I'm sorry, truly sorry, for my selfishness. I believe that in order for you to accept Nicolas, you need to close the circle that I have broken. I have enclosed the only picture I have of your father, Barnibus Grant, along with his last known address. As far as I know, he still lives there. This may be too little too late and may cause more problems for you. I'm only sorry that you could not hear this from my own lips. I love you, Ieshelle, and pray that you can forgive me. I pray that you don't make the same mistake I did. Your baby needs his father, just like you need yours.

Love, Mom

◆ ◆ ◆

I let the letter drift to the table as tears blurred my eyes. How could she . . . how could she keep this from me? I covered my face with my hands, trying to contemplate everything that my mother had revealed to me. *What just happened here?*

Forty-Eight

Three days after Ieshelle told me good-bye, three days since the memorial service for her mother, had been three days of hell. Nicolette and my mother tried to reassure me that Ieshelle just needed time. I hoped they were right. I was dying without her. I had been working out so much and running that I had lost too much weight. Frank had to switch my workout schedule, and I had to see a dietician so that I could put some weight back on before the fight.

Tony continued to give me daily updates on Ieshelle's whereabouts and safety. There still had been no sign of Damien. The report he handed me on the guy only made me want to kick his ass more. After Ieshelle had escaped him, Damien had several girlfriends, all of whom left him after being victims of his physical and sexual abuse. All of the women had been in their twenties, except one who was nineteen. They all had something in common—they had no family here in the States or no family at all. None of the women lived in Las Vegas currently, as all had fled to different parts of the country to escape Damien.

I learned that Damien had been the promotional executive for one of the big local hotels for the past six years. There was one incident about eight years ago with a secretary who accused him of sexual assault, but she later recanted and moved out of the city. Tony also found that Damien's bank accounts had far more money than he should have on his salary. Tony suspected that he was taking kickbacks from certain companies as incentive to promote their products or businesses at the hotel. Tony wasn't able to locate Damien at the moment. Every time he called or stopped by his office, he was unavailable. There also weren't any recent paper trails for him to follow. It was as if he disappeared off the face of the earth.

I looked down in disgust at the plate of food I was attempting to eat. I didn't have an appetite. That had added to the weight loss. I had so much pent-up energy right now that I felt like taking a run. Frank had cut from my workout anything that burned calories fast and had added more agility and strengthening exercises. I sometimes completed workouts in the pool— the aquatic training after my injury had been beneficial, and Frank and I had incorporated it into my regular routine.

In addition to the public appearances and meetings with promoters and sponsors, I was still studying my lines for the upcoming movie and working with the stunt coordinator. I couldn't deny my excitement about the movie; it would be the first of many—I just knew it.

I constantly thought of how everything in my life could mesh with everything in Ieshelle's, but I had to have a solid plan if I was going to convince her that our relationship could work. I smiled at that thought. Up until now, I had been thinking in past tense, as if we would never be together again. This was the first time that the confidence I usually felt in combat had returned. I would have to fight with everything I had for Ieshelle. *Patience is a virtue,* I thought, *one I hope I have mastered.*

Forty-Nine

I stood outside the house, trying to work up the nerve to knock on the door. The estate was intimidating, and I thought I must have gotten the directions wrong when I turned into the drive of the prestigious home. The wrought-iron gate and manicured lawns bespoke wealth and station. A woman with a deep Jamaican accent buzzed me through the gates. The sound of her voice caused my eyes to tear as memories of my mother surfaced, her voice comforting in its welcome.

I couldn't sleep after I read the letter but had to wait until this morning to attempt to trace my father's whereabouts. It had been remarkably easy, and by the time I got directions to the estate it was dinnertime. I hoped that he was at home, as I couldn't wait until tomorrow. I carried the picture in my hand, along with the letter my mother had left me. I was just about to leave when the door swung open. I stepped back as a woman looked at me curiously and then beckoned me to enter.

"You come right on in, miss. We been waiting for you for a long time, we have. Is your mother with you?" She looked behind me expectantly.

I shook my head, the sadness of her passing once again filling me. I looked back to her face once again, this time in shock—*waiting for me?* But my mother said my father didn't know about me. How could they have been expecting me?

"Mr. Grant is just sitting to supper in the dining room. Please follow me. My name is Annabel, but you call me Anna, child." Her accent was even heavier than my mother's, and the sound of it reminded me so much of her that my eyes began to water again.

"I'm sorry, I didn't . . . I don't want to disturb his dinner. I can come back."

"Oh no, miss. You won't be disturbing Mr. Grant at all. He always have a place at the table for you and your mother. He been hoping you would come for some fifteen years now. You have your mother's eyes, that's how I knew it was you at the door. I remember the first time I saw Ms. Sophie. She was like a breath of fresh air, she was. She breathed life back into us. Back into my Barnie. No, you come on in. Mr. Grant would have my head if I let you outta here before he got to see you. He been waiting an awful long time to meet his only daughter."

I stumbled a moment and had to catch myself. *If he knew, then why hadn't he contacted me?* I didn't understand. I started to back out of the door, thinking this was a big mistake, when a tall gentleman with a fair complexion and steel-gray eyes stepped into the foyer. He had an intelligent face, a smart nose, and aristocratic jaw. He smiled softly, showing even white teeth. He was about Nicolas's height and had the physique of one who kept physically active. His hair waved on his crown in dark ebony curls, with only a slight graying at the temples, which gave him a distinguished appearance. He wore black slacks and a crisp white dress shirt with a black, gray, and red diagonally striped tie paired with a gray sweater that brought out the color in his eyes. He stepped forward in welcome, but I was full of nerves and had the urge to flee. Something, however, held me in place—his eyes; they looked at me with longing and unquestionable love.

"I have waited a long time for this day." His voice was strong and soothed my nerves. "I'm sorry to hear that your mother did not accompany you, I had hoped . . ." He looked off into the distance, as if she would appear behind me. His eyes glazed over momentarily before he continued. "No worries. Please be easy. No one here means you any harm."

"I . . . my mother . . .Sophie...are you . . .?" I stuttered.

"My name is Barnabus Grant, and I believe I am your father," he stated simply.

"How do you know that?"

"Come in. Let's sit and have dinner, and I will tell you everything you want to know. And maybe you will tell me something about yourself and your mother, Sophie, also." His voice was wistful . . . hopeful.

It pained me to confirm that she was gone; they would never have their second chance. I realized then that I hadn't introduced myself. "I'm sorry—how rude of me. My name is Ieshelle . . . Ieshelle Jones."

He held his hand out to me, and I placed mine in his. His grip was strong and reassuring as he placed my hand on his elbow and escorted me to the dining room.

◆ ◆ ◆

We sat down at a cherry wood double-pedestal table that was set for three but probably could seat twelve. He sat at the head of the table, and I sat to his right, the empty seating on his left side. Ecru-colored linen covered the table, and silver candelabra were spaced down the center. The three place settings were beautiful white china with gold trim and a royal-looking insignia in the middle of the plates.

The walls of the dining room were painted a warm honey color, and there were small bowls of peach roses on the buffet and in the center of the table that completed the decor. A beautiful crystal chandelier hung from the ceiling, providing ambient light. I took a deep breath and asked the first question that came to mind.

"How did you find out about me?"

"I searched everywhere for your mother, after she left me, but she seemed to have disappeared. I figured she must have changed her name, which you confirmed for me. Sophie's last name was Jameson when I met her. Did she marry?" When I shook my head, he continued. "I discovered later it was eight years before she set foot back on this island, and by then, I had returned to Britain, having given up on ever seeing her again, I tried to move on with my life. I married and have one son, Benjamin, but I just could not stay away from the island. When my wife passed after her battle with cancer, I returned. I learned that your mother had lived here with her daughter for ten years before moving to the States. I also learned that your brother was killed after being caught in the crossfire of a gang fight. No one was sure where you had settled, and the private investigator could not find a paper trail. When I heard about the little girl and her description, I knew that girl was —my daughter. I prayed that one day you would come here in search of the truth."

I was overcome by sudden awareness as I looked again at the three place settings. "Have you been . . . setting a place for me and my mother at your table for the past fifteen years?"

He nodded, and when he spoke, his voice caught in this throat. "Yes, I . . . I have. I had hoped . . ."

Anna entered with two bowls of steaming soup, placing them before us, adding a single peach-colored rose on top of the place setting that had been meant for my mother before returning to the kitchen.

I smiled at the thoughtfulness before inhaling the aroma of the soup—a rich lobster bisque, one of my favorites—and we ate in silence as I contemplated all he had said. The watchful Anna came back to pick up the dishes as soon as we'd finished and informed us that the entrée would be ready shortly. I took a sip of the white wine that had been served with the dish before asking another question that had been plaguing me. "What happened between you and my mother?" The letter had given a glimpse into the turmoil but didn't explain what happened.

"Your mother was the love of my life," he confessed easily. I looked at him in shock, remembering that he had married. "I did care for my late wife, but I could never love her the way that I loved your mother. She understood that. To answer your question, I would have to start at the beginning . . ."

I took another sip of wine and nodded, encouraging him to begin.

"I met Sophie in the local market one day. She was selling her paintings and various other crafts, and I was drawn to one picture in particular—it was of this very house. We started talking about the painting and from there it just kind of took off. The house had come to me from my uncle Etienne Grant, who in fact was an earl. He took me in after my parents were killed in a plane crash when I was seven, and he raised me as his son and heir—he had no wife or children of his own. I came here to escape and heal from the grief of losing him—he died of a sudden heart attack—I thought I was all alone until I met your mother."

He stared off into the distance, as if remembering the very moment, as he continued. "She was like a breath of fresh air. She rejuvenated me and filled me with such joy and happiness. I had never met anyone like her; she was a free spirit. Things didn't fall apart between us until I told her I owned this house. That seemed to change everything. She spoke some nonsense about people like me not marrying people like her. It wasn't a race issue as much as it was a station issue. Sophie felt that we were from two different worlds, and she didn't believe that she belonged in mine. She felt like she wasn't good enough for me." He looked back at me then, his eyes pleading with me to understand. "No matter what I did, she wouldn't change her mind. I realized later that it was hard to break what she had witnessed all her life—that nothing was free. She felt that I would pay too high a price for having an uneducated black woman as my wife—her words, not mine. I didn't care about her lack of formal education. I loved her; that was enough for me. Your mother was very stubborn, Ieshelle, but one night, when I had laid everything out to her again—my plans for our future and our family—she gave herself to me. I thought she finally understood and had changed her mind, but I was wrong. Instead of her saying yes to our future, she actually had been saying good-bye." He grew quiet.

"I'm sorry," I said softly, remembering Anna's words from earlier and hearing the love coloring his voice. He truly loved my mother, as his whole countenance changed with him just reminiscing of her. "I'm sorry that so much time was wasted and that you will never—" I whispered, my voice tight with emotion at that reality.

"Never?" His voice quavered with the word, as if finally comprehending.

"She recently passed away," I explained.

A tear slid unchecked down his cheek, and he grew silent. I felt I had to say something. "She, like you, was never able to truly love completely again, her heart still belonged to you." I shared. "I can understand what she was feeling. I myself have had similar notions rather recently, to be honest." He looked up at me with renewed interest as I voiced my next question. "Why did she believe you had so much to lose?"

"I was a dignitary, and the son of an earl. I could have run for chancellor if I'd chosen to do so. Sophie felt that my career would suffer as a result of our relationship."

Anna entered with the entrée—a mouth-watering herb- crusted salmon—along with fresh green beans and garlic mashed potatocs. Silence permeated again as we ate, but when the plates were finally taken away, I asked the question that had been niggling at me. "So, what now?"

"Well, that depends on you, Ieshelle. I know it is too late for you to need a father, but I would like the chance to get to know you. I would very much like to be a part of your life, if you will have me."

The words were so similar to those that Nicolas had spoken that I realized at that moment I had made a monumental mistake. I was doing the same thing that my mother had done to my father, and if my mother was right—as I suspected she was—I was pregnant with Nicolas's child right now. I reached across the table to grab my father's hand, needing his strength, needing his love. It was not too late for us, and I prayed that it was not too late for Nicolas and me.

"I still need you," I assured him, "In spite of what you might think. I need you in my life." I confessed.

He stood then, pulling me to my feet to engulf me in his warm, loving embrace. He smelled like a comforting spice blend, smoky vanilla, and I felt safe within his arms. We spent the remainder of the night talking, and I told him about everything—from Damien, to my business ventures, to Nicolas, to my current predicament. I shared the letter my mother wrote to me, along with his faded picture. We talked for hours and lost track of time. Before we knew, it was past midnight.

My father insisted that I stay over. "You can return home in the morning," he said, "After breakfast."

I was more than happy to oblige, because I really didn't want to go back to the empty house. I had realized something else—I was not alone. I had my father.

And I prayed that I still had Nicolas.

Fifty

FIGHT NIGHT

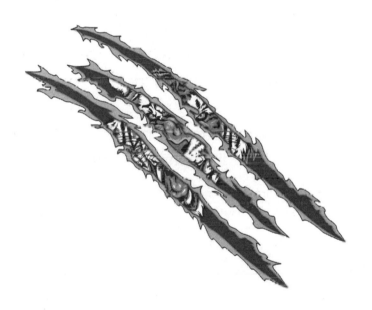

T he city buzzed with excitement as celebrities and high- rollers filled the streets, hotels, and clubs. I closed my eyes, leaning my head back against the wall as I attempted to temper the power that vibrated throughout my being. The day had finally come.

I would reclaim my title and restore myself in the eyes of my fans and sponsors—except all I could think about was whether or not I could restore myself in Ieshelle's eyes.

I shouldn't have left her, but her rejection had been like a knife stabbing me in the heart. *What more did she want from me? What more was I willing to endure?* Anything. Everything, I answered myself. I would endure anything for Ieshelle. I thought about what Nicolette and my mother had practically drilled in my head. I pushed her. It was too much, too soon.

Patience. I was learning to respect that word even more. If I hadn't been so consumed with passion and the desire to claim her, I would have recognized that it was too much for her. In fact, I had recognized it, but I'd run roughshod over her anyway, thinking that my love for her would be enough to smooth out everything. I fucked up.

I turned the music up, attempting to block out the sounds of the personnel who surrounded me. I was supposed to be focusing on the fight. Mark Hiden. The one who had forced me into submission and cost me my title. I had been so angry at him at first, but now, I realized that if it hadn't been for that loss, I never would have met Ieshelle again. Fate was having her way with me. Probably laughing at the mess I had made of things.

Ieshelle had returned from Jamaica yesterday. As soon as Tony called, I had been intent on rushing over to her. It was only after I was sitting behind the wheel that I stopped myself. I was doing it again—pushing when I should just wait. But damn, how long would it take? It was killing me not waking up to her warm smile, to her eyes still hooded with sleep. I felt like I was losing my mind, listening for her laugh, one that had come so freely. I had grown to love it and took pride in being the one to have caused the return of that laughter. I wanted to hold her, kiss her, and tell her I loved her. I missed hearing her voice.

I hadn't called her. Not one time since she left Las Vegas. I was trying to give her the space that I had failed to provide her initially. I got up to start stretching, putting my body through the paces as I prepared to enter the ring. I needed to expend some energy, and I still had another preliminary bout to wait before my fight.

I couldn't help thinking about Ieshelle. What could I do to get her back? Maybe if I wooed her again—flowers, candy, cards? Hell, we hadn't even been out on a date before the first night we made love. Realizing that fact, I felt like an idiot. The Mothers Against Domestic Violence event didn't really count, as she was already set to attend.

I resolved to correct everything that I had done wrong with Ieshelle. I would help her to grow comfortable with my feelings for her and more important, with her feelings for me. She needed to regain confidence in her ability to make decisions about her life. I wouldn't give up on us, and I wouldn't let her give up on us either. I would just change my tactics. One thing I wasn't was a quitter.

Fifty-One

Fight Night

T he city was alive with people roaming the streets as they took in the sights before attending the big event tonight. I closed the office early, as some of the staff wanted to prepare for the parties and others wanted to get home to avoid the traffic. I looked in the mirror as Eedie finished applying her makeup. I was nervous, although I didn't know why. Yes, I did. I have been back from Jamaica for one full day, and I haven't talked to Nicolas yet. I didn't know what to say.

It had taken me hours to decide what to wear. I settled on a yellow and nude McCartney dress that gave the illusion I wasn't wearing anything beneath and left most of my back bare. I carried a navy Burch mini tote, and because it was quite windy tonight, I wore a navy Grant mid-thigh trench coat. I accessorized the ensemble with lapis drop earrings, a matching cluster bubble bib necklace, and couture hinge bangle. The shoe candy for tonight were my red-bottom navy snakeskin peep-toe pumps. I took my time with my makeup, going for a simple eye-shadow effect of coordinating golds and browns with a bright red lip.

As I looked at Eedie in the mirror, I thought of how much had changed for her in such a short time. Earlier, she had told me about her small baby bump she was now sporting. I couldn't help the pang in my heart, remembering the joy I had experienced when I thought I was expecting Nicolas's baby and the sharp pain of disappointment when it was proven false. I thought about my mother's prediction and involuntarily ran a hand over my still-flat stomach. Eden Rose had taken a chance on Jacob, and look at her now—happily married and expecting her first baby. She was a doctor and career woman and now worked as one of the on-call docs on the professional racecar circuit. She had given up her job in Dallas, where she had worked as an ER doctor, to be with Jacob. Was I brave enough to do the same?

"I can't wait to meet Nicolas," Eedie said enthusiastically. "You do love him, Shelly, don't you?"

"Yes, but—"

"Then that's it—no more buts! If you love him, you have to find a way to make it work. Trust me, Shelly. If he loves you as much as you say, then you grab hold of him and fight for what you can have. Running only wastes time, and life is not promised to us—it's too short."

I nodded, understanding where she was coming from. As a professional stock-car driver, Jacob risked his life every time he got behind the wheel, just as Nicolas risked his life every time he stepped into the ring. Eden Rose was right—life was too short. My mother's recent death was testament to that fact.

Jacob knocked on the door then, signaling that the car had arrived to pick us up. Brian and Alexis were to join us. It was their first outing alone since the birth of their son four months ago. They were a beautiful couple. Alexis had bright golden eyes and chocolate-brown skin; Brian was fair, with deep blue eyes and golden hair. It was quite harrowing, watching the couple— an unconscious caress . . . a gentle touch. The same was for Jacob and Eden Rose. They unconsciously gravitated towards one another. The more time I spent with each couple, the more I yearned for what they had. I just had to figure out a way. Besides, there was more than just me to think about now . . . if my mother's prediction was correct.

Fifty-Two

The beast was back and in full form—I annihilated Mark Hiden. I won my title back by TKO in the third round, and the shit felt good! I had removed the albatross from my neck, and now it was time to get my woman. I dressed quickly in the black slacks and a matching dress shirt, prepared for the after-parties we would attend tonight to celebrate my win. I looked at myself in the mirror again, even as I held the ice pack to my left eye in an attempt to ease the slight swelling from the few blows that Hiden was able to get in. I didn't want Ieshelle to be alarmed by the sight of me.

I noticed her sitting in the third row, center. Ieshelle was ravishing, and the yellow lace dress she wore hugged all of her curves, its crafted illusion giving the impression that her womanly attributes were barely covered. The sparkle had returned to her eyes, and a smile graced her lips, all of it directed at me. *Damn*, I missed her!

I recognized Eden Rose and her husband, Jacob. They were sitting with Alexis and Brian, the obvious love and affection they had for each other evident in every touch and smile. I wanted that for me, but more important, I wanted it for Ieshelle too. She deserved to be happy. She deserved to feel loved, and I would spend the rest of my days making sure she did just that.

The fact that she'd come to the fight tonight had to be a sign that she still loved me . . . *didn't it?* I hated feeling so confused and on edge. Never had a woman caused me to be tied up with nerves like Ieshelle.

Hope filled my heart as I took another look in the mirror, still noting some puffiness to my eye. I felt like it was as good as it was going to get, and I headed out, anxious to find her.

Fifty-Three

I leaned up against the wall outside of the locker rooms. I was standing amongst all the reporters and groupies that were vying for the fighters' attentions. I almost left when I saw how many women whose demeanor were practically screaming that they were available. My confidence slipped by several degrees; maybe I had waited too long. I sent Eedie and the others ahead of me, saying I would meet up with them at the party later. Now, I wasn't entirely sure that was true. I really fucked this up! I had just turned to leave when someone grabbed my right arm—painfully. I looked up and was shocked to see familiar green eyes staring back at me. Damien!

"What are you doing here?" Then I took note of his appearance—he was wearing a security shirt similar to those worn by the staff of the arena. What was he up to? "Let me go Damien!" I said as I attempted to wrench my arm free.

That only infuriated him and he squeezed my arm harder until tears sprang to my eyes. He pulled me to him so that my back was to his chest and covered my mouth with his gloved hand. His eyes were wild, and he smelled strongly of alcohol. I looked around for help, trying to gain eye contact with anyone. A large black man, slightly smaller in stature than Nicolas, was headed my way when two burly security guards attempted to detained him. He was pointing his finger toward me, before he dropped the two guards with a quick move. Three more guards quickly replaced those downed, and I then heard Damien laugh.

"Your hired muscle is spitting mad that the arena security won't let him through, especially since I gave his description to them as a potential threat."

"My hired muscle?" I mumbled stupidly behind his hand. *What was he talking about?* Damien ushered me through the thick crowd in the opposite direction from where my "hired muscle" was being detained. Damien kept his head low, close to my neck, so that we didn't look conspicuous. I didn't think anyone would notice anything in this crowd, as people were swarming in an attempt to get closer, to see the fighters when they emerged from the locker rooms. The security detail had their hands full already.

"So, your boyfriend didn't tell you he has been paying for you to have round-the-clock security since I was released from jail."

I was unable to fathom what he was saying. *Nicolas had paid for an around the clock security detail? Even after I told him no?* I stumbled a little as the crowd pressed in on us, and I realized that the fighters must have emerged because deafening cheers and applause filled the hall. I did my best to struggle, hoping to slow, Damien down. I prayed that Nicolas would spot us or that my security guard would break free before we rounded the corner.

Fifty-Four

I stepped out into the hall, immediately searching the crowd for Ieshelle. One of the arena security guys said he saw a woman fitting her description hanging out in the hall with the reporters. He stated it was hard to miss her in the stunning yellow dress. I growled my displeasure and he quickly pointed me in the direction that he had seen her. I tried to get

Frank and Jacque to get her cleared to the back, but they couldn't locate her after the match.

I fielded a few interviews and used the time to continue to study the crowd. *Where the hell is she?* Apprehension filled me, and for some reason, I knew inexplicably that something was wrong. That's when I noticed that Tony was being held against the nearest wall by four security guys, all of whom were sporting bloody noses and swelling eyes. I headed in his direction, directing the security guys to let him go.

"No can do, Nico. There was a report that a guy of his physical description was a potential threat, and he has been a royal pain in the ass since we detained him."

"Yeah, the bastard broke my nose!" one of the other security guys piped in.

"This is my fiancée's private security guard," I snapped. I looked at Tony, and saw concern and alarm evident in his eyes.

"He has her!" Tony shouted as he immediately started looking into the crowd.

I didn't need to ask who; there was only one man I feared hurting Ieshelle—Damien. "Where are they?"

Tony pointed toward the end of the hall that led from the arena. That's when I spotted them moving in the crowd, with Ieshelle doing her best to slow him down. I instructed the security guards to radio for help as there was an attempted kidnapping in progress, and all exits needed to be sealed. I prayed that someone was already stationed at the exit door at the end of the hall. I instructed the others to follow Tony and me as we moved through the crowd as swiftly as we could in pursuit. My heart was pounding in my chest as fear and adrenaline spurred me on. I wouldn't let him hurt her again. I would stop him or die trying.

Fifty-Five

I stumbled again as Damien continued to pull me along the corridor. My wrist was throbbing, and my fingers were numb. All I felt from the area was an intense, burning pain. As we got closer to the corner, the crowd thinned out, our footsteps echoed against the walls. Where was he taking me? He had to have made a plan, because he was dressed in the security get up. Obviously, he wasn't thinking rationally.

"Your boyfriend thinks he's the shit!" Damien snarled. "Do you know that motherfucker got me fired? *Me!* Damien Brooks!" I shook my head in denial—that didn't sound like Nicolas; if anything, I would have suspected him of breaking Damien's nose or jaw. My response seemed to anger Damien, as he tightened his hold.

"My boss said that someone came to the office several times inquiring about me. Someone also left several messages. The person apparently looked very official, maybe even a federal agent. Those inquiries prompted an investigation. They accused me of misappropriation of funds and bribery."

Paralyzing fear ran down my back as I listened to Damien. It was very possible that Nicolas had nothing to do with Damien's job, but Damien assumed he had. I wondered if I was Damien's original target—or if it had been Nicolas. I suspected he had to have a concealed weapon. He wouldn't attack Nicolas outright.

"I know it has to be your little boyfriend behind this. He's probably the reason that some of my suppliers chose new hotels to offer their products. I lost a lot of money because of him."

I realized then that Damien was clearly unstable, and maybe alcohol was not the only thing he had been imbibing.

"You know, I thought you had escaped me. Went by your house for days with no activity, so when I saw you there in the hallway, waiting for him like a bitch in heat, I knew what I had to do. You were the cause of all this. If I eliminate you, I will eliminate my problem!"

He had been watching my house? The thought made me sick to my stomach, but it also explained why Nicolas had hired the security guard. Damien slowed down to check the side doors to see if they were open. When he momentarily loosened his grip on my arm, I shoved back against him and wrenched my wrist hard, breaking free. I ran toward the hallway we had come from. I could hear Damien in pursuit, cursing behind me, but I had a good head start.

I thought I heard footsteps up ahead when some instinct told me to duck. I dropped down low, just as a shot rang out, and the blast from the gun lit the hallway. *Oh, my God, he has a gun!* I was close to one of the doors Damien had found locked, but I pushed on it anyway and was surprised when it suddenly opened. I fell into a room that was filled with large, unfamiliar equipment. I skinned my knee on the floor but recovered and looked for a place to hide.

I located another door, but it was locked. I was about to double back when I heard the door I entered creak. It was dark in the room— only a sliver of light coming from the bottom of the door allowed me to see anything. When the door swung open, I immediately ducked down. It closed again shortly afterward, and I did my best to calm my breathing, but I was shaking so hard, I felt like I was making too much noise. Tears welled in my eyes as I inched farther behind a large piece of equipment. I could hear footsteps getting closer to me, the ominous sound filling the void. I held my breath—it felt as if he was standing right over me. Suddenly, the door was wrenched open, and I heard loud voices.

"I saw him come in here, Nicolas!"

"Okay, we need to fan out. Billy said the police radioed that they are on the premises, and he gave them our latest location. Be careful; we now know that he is armed."

Nicolas! If that was him entering now that meant Damien had entered previously. Someone was holding the door open, because the light continued to filter into the room, but in spite of its addition, it remained relatively dark, with only a small pool of light brightening the doorway. I looked around, trying to detect where Damien was. There was only one way in and one way out, as the other door in the room was locked. I concentrated on taking slow breaths so that I wasn't hyperventilating, and I held my throbbing wrist to my chest. I couldn't move it without sharp pains shooting up my arm, and I was scared that it was broken. I heard a noise to the left and held my breath, praying that it was Nicolas but having a premonition that Damien would step into the light.

Fifty-Six

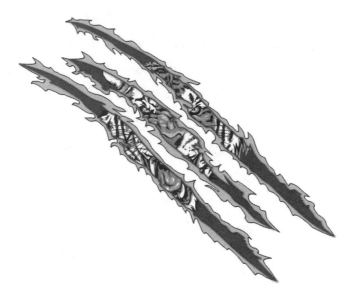

I looked frantically around the room. Somehow, I knew Ieshelle was in here. I hadn't seen her enter, but I hadn't heard her footsteps either after we saw Damien enter this room. *Shit!*

He has a gun! This shit could go bad real fast. The room was large, and the light from the door really didn't help. I hadn't heard any movement either; maybe Tony got it wrong. Billy tried the light switch but nothing happened. I was just about to call the others back when I felt something under my foot and discovered a woman's earring—a blue lapis earring, if I was right. Damn. Ieshelle had been wearing blue and yellow tonight, and I would bet anything that it was hers.

I flagged everyone, signaling to keep quiet. I held up the earring, letting them know that Ieshelle was also in here. If Damien didn't have her right now, we weren't going to let him know that she was hiding. I looked back to the door where Billy stood watch, waiting for the police to arrive. *Why wasn't Damien firing at them?* He had to know we were in here, that it was only a matter of time before we found him.

No sooner had the thought crossed my mind than a shot rang out. The bullet was so close that I felt the heat it caused as it whizzed by my ear. The flash from the gun indicated his position, and I shouted to the others, "Get down! He's to the left." I could hear shuffling and slowly advanced in the opposite direction. I assumed Damien would be trying to adjust his position. If he was on the left, Ieshelle was most likely on the right, so I had to be quick. It was darker on this side of the room, and there seemed to be several large pieces of equipment stationed here. I stopped for a moment . . . I thought I heard something. I moved back and peered behind the last piece of equipment I passed and found Ieshelle huddled there holding her hand to her chest.

I knelt down and took her into my arms. She was trembling, and silent tears trailed down her cheeks. I took a calming breath, trying to steal the fury and anxiety that was raging in me. I had to get her out of here. Her shoes and handbag were on the floor. I grabbed both with one hand, tucking the earring I held into my pocket as I helped her up. I hoped the boys had cornered Damien on the far side of the room and we could make it out the door.

I heard the distinct click of a gun before we had even taken a step. Suddenly, the room was flooded with overhead light, blinding me momentarily, but the police swarmed in, and I could see Tony and the security guys retreating at their direction.

"Don't move!" one of the officers shouted to Damien. "Put down your weapon!"

Damien continued to stare to the right of me, where Ieshelle stood. He had a deranged look in his eyes, and I knew he wasn't going to go down without a fight. I saw his finger twitch on the trigger of the gun, and with a burst of speed, I attempted to block Ieshelle, his intended target. The gun fired simultaneously with my ramming into Ieshelle. I did my best to take the brunt of the fall. Seconds later, the police fired consecutive shots, and I heard a loud thud as Damien fell to the floor.

As I lay there, dazed from the impact, I felt a burning sensation along my right bicep and saw bright red blood oozing through my shirt sleeve. It felt like my arm was on fire. *Shit, Ieshelle!* I sat up, removing my weight, to realize that she wasn't moving. *Damn, had she hit her head in the fall?* "Ieshelle, baby, are you hurt?" I asked, looking down into her face. Her eyes were closed and she was so still . . . I panicked momentarily, until I felt her warm breath against my cheek. But before I could even sigh in relief that she was alive, I noticed the blood trailing from her head. *No! Please, God, no! I can't lose her now!* I scrambled to my knees in front of her and ripped off my shirt, using it to apply pressure to her wound. I vaguely heard the police calling for an ambulance as I cradled Ieshelle in my arms, tears streaming down my face.

Fifty-Seven

My heart nearly jumped out of my chest at the sound of gunfire, and I almost ran out in search of Nicolas. *Oh God, please don't let Damien hurt him,* I thought. I placed my good hand over my mouth in an attempt to keep quiet as I scooted farther behind the large piece of equipment. I had removed my shoes, not wanting to alert Damien to my position if I had to move. I took some deep breaths, holding my injured hand across my chest to ease the pain. My fingertips were numb, and a constant throbbing radiated up my arm from my wrist.

I heard shuffling as people moved around. I held my breath as I heard footsteps moving closer to me, and when a dark figure loomed over me, I froze. I expected that at any second, the gun would fire, ending my life. In that moment, all I could think of was that I never got to tell Nicolas I was sorry. I never told him that I loved him and that I wanted us to be together. I'd wasted time, and now my time was up.

Suddenly, the figure knelt down before me. I moved to scoot back, all the while reaching for one of my shoes. It would afford some protection, even if infitesimal. I caught a glimpse of his silhouette. There was something familiar about the profile. *Nicolas!* I started shaking uncontrollably as relief flooded over me. *Nicolas is here!*

I was swiftly wrapped into strong arms, and I could feel warm tears trail down my cheeks. We had to get out of here! Before we could even move a step, I heard the distinct click of a gun.

Suddenly, the room was flooded with overhead light, blinding me. The police swarmed into the room, and one shouted, "Don't move! Put down your weapon!"

I could see Damien now, and he stared at me, his eyes burning with hatred. He was a crazed madman and far past any reasoning. I saw Damien's finger twitch. An instant later, the gun fired. Nicolas knocked me to the floor in an effort to shield me from the impact. I did my best to suck air into my lungs, but my chest hurt, and my head was throbbing—*I think I hit my head on the floor after I fell.* Seconds later, consecutive shots were fired—I assumed it was the police—and then a loud thud from the direction where Damien had been standing.

I lay there, dazed from the impact, with my eyes blurring and the room spinning. I could hear Nicolas say something to me, and I tried to answer him, but everything went dark. It was as if huge weights had been placed on my eyelids as pressure continued to build in my head. I tried to move my hands to let him know I was okay, but I couldn't seem to get them to work. Pressure continued to build behind my eyes, and the pain grew in intensity until it was a constant throbbing.

I could hear Nicolas screaming my name over and over again, begging me not to leave him. *I am right here,* I tried to say. *I will never leave you again if you give me another chance.* But the pain was becoming too much, and the darkness enveloped me.

Fifty-Eight

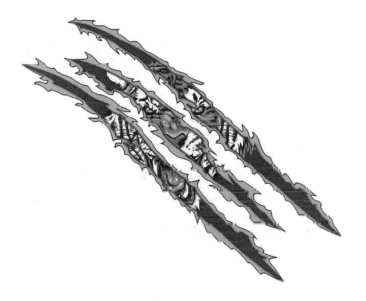

I held Ieshelle to my chest as I applied pressure to her head. My shirt was already soaked with blood, and I could feel the sticky wetness coating my hand. There was so much of it! I kept her positioned so that I could feel her breath against my neck, assuring me she was still alive. I didn't realize that I had been rocking back and forth with her. Moments which felt like an eternity later, I felt someone attempt to pull Ieshelle from my arms. I held her tighter, unable to make out who stood there, as my vision was blurred.

"Nicolas, it's just the paramedics," someone said. "Nicolas, they just want to help her."

"Frank?"

"Yeah, it's me. Jacque is here too. We're all really worried about Ieshelle, Nicolas. The paramedics won't hurt her. Just let them look at her."

I nodded then, swiping at my tears as I allowed them to lift Ieshelle to the waiting stretcher. I looked at my hands then, covered with her blood, and felt my stomach roil. As I took deep breaths to get myself under control, a paramedic stepped up to me looking concerned. "Sir, you should let us look at your arm. You're bleeding pretty badly."

I shook my head no, having forgotten the injury to my arm when I realized that Ieshelle had been shot in the head.

◆ ◆ ◆

The ride to the hospital was the longest ride of my life. The paramedics worked frantically on Ieshelle once they loaded her into the ambulance. I tried to answer the questions they asked to the best of my ability, but I was no good. I couldn't see past the blood on my hands, although the paramedics assured me that she was still breathing on her own and was stable.

Once we reached the hospital, I was stopped in the waiting room to fill out paperwork while they took Ieshelle back to triage. There was also the wound to my arm that had to be stitched and bandaged which took about half an hour. They let me back later for short visits in between different tests. Ieshelle's eyes were always closed but the last time I visited, she actually moved voluntarily. Frank, Jacque, and Tony had followed the ambulance to the hospital. I couldn't sit still; I left the room after they took Ieshelle for yet another test. I was pacing the hall when the doctor emerged from behind the double doors. Everything moved in slow motion as she approached us. I ran my hand over my head in frustration, the bandage on my arm pulling slightly, reminding me of my own injury.

"Is the family for Ieshelle Jones here?"

"Yes," I said, stepping forward. Frank, Jacque, and Tony flanked me. "I'm her fiancé, Nicolas St. Pierre." I informed as I stared at her curiously, wondering what happened to the other doctor.

"I'm Dr. Bartholomew, Dr. Sellers is now in surgery with another patient. Your fiancée is resting comfortably now. She required a few stitches. The bullet grazed her just above the right brow to her temple. Head wounds tend to bleed more than other wounds, so it looked far worse than it actually was. We were concerned that she hadn't regained consciousness when she arrived at the ER, but that has since resolved, and she is now awake and alert. We have watched her for the last few hours, and aside from pain at the site which is expected, she is stable. All of her diagnostic tests have come back normal. She was also able to rest with some pain medication. We expect a full recovery."

I let out the breath I hadn't realized I'd been holding. *She's going to be okay!*

"There is another condition, however," Dr. Bartholomew said, looking uncomfortable, "Of which I assume you are unaware—you didn't include the information when you filled out her paperwork. It is still very early on...we actually only discovered it because we had to be sure due to some other tests we needed to perform."

"What are you talking about? What kind of condition?"

"Mr. St. Pierre, your fiancé is pregnant. You can go back and see her now," she answered. "Everyone is going to be all right, with enough rest." Her pager went off. "I have to take this. If you have any questions, just have the nurse page me." And with that she was off to answer the call.

What the hell was she talking about? 'Everyone is going to be okay.' What does that mean? I turned as I suddenly heard the snickering behind me. "Just what the hell is so bloody funny?" I demanded of Frank and Jacque.

"Maybe you hit *your* head, Nico." Jacque stated.

"She said, Ieshelle's is pregnant," Frank supplied.

"Pregnant? But . . . I don't understand."

"Well, obviously you understood something, or you wouldn't be in this predicament," Tony piped in, his face softened with humor. I glared at them as I walked away. *Ieshelle . . . pregnant?*

Fifty-Nine

I lay on my side, staring at the wall. I was still somewhat in shock over the whole ordeal. Damien was dead. The police had shot him after he fired the gun at me. Nicolas did his best to block the shot, but the bullet still managed to graze my forehead. I ran my hand over the dressing that covered the wound. My head was no longer pounding, like it was when I first came in, thanks to those lovely IV meds. Now there was only a dull ache. Still, it was a constant reminder of how close I had come to death. I thought this night would be so different. I had hoped . . . I had hoped that Nicolas and I could reconcile, but now. . . I couldn't help the sobs that burst free. I'd messed up everything.

I heard the door creak and I turned over, expecting to see the nurse returning with my discharge papers.

Nicolas stood inside the room, his face unreadable. *Was he still angry with me?* Hurt? I had left him not once but twice. I had rejected him over and over, without a care for his feelings, only thinking of protecting my own. I began sobbing again, afraid it was too late for us.

"Please don't cry, *ange*," Nicolas whispered as he crossed the distance. His fingers trailed against my cheeks, brushing the errant drops away.

"Nicolas . . . I . . . I had so much to say before . . . I wanted to tell you . . . You know, don't you?" My heart clenched as I awaited his response.

He nodded. I turned back toward the wall, afraid that I would see condemnation in his eyes. Moments later, I felt the bed dipping as

Nicolas lay beside me. He pulled me into his arms and adjusted our position so that my head was pillowed on his chest.

"Shhh, *ange.* Tell me what's wrong. Talk to me," Nicolas instructed as he gently rubbed his hand along my back.

I sniffed. "I don't know where to start."

"We have plenty of time, Ieshelle. There is no rush."

I relaxed at his words and found comfort in his embrace. "My mother knew everything, Nicolas, and yet she made the same mistake I made with you."

"What do you mean?"

I rubbed my jaw against his chest unconsciously. His heart pounded in my ears, and I trailed my hand across his abdomen.

"I found my father."

"What?"

"He lives in Jamaica on a beautiful estate. I told him that I would bring you back to meet him, but that was before . . ." I broke off as the sadness consumed me again.

"What are you talking about? Hey, hey, calm down."

"That was before all this stuff with Damien again . . . and then I never got to tell you what I found out. And now you know about the baby . . . six weeks exactly—I just found out today. You probably think I'm trying to trap you, but it's nothing like that. Well, I would if I could, because I love you, but that would be wrong, especially if you don't love me anymore. I think I blew it big time . . ." I knew I was rambling, but I couldn't seem to stop.

It was as if everything was pouring out on fast-forward, and I couldn't slow down.

Nicolas leaned down suddenly, his lips covering mine in a dominating kiss, effectively silencing me. His lips brushed across mine over and over again, begging for entrance into my mouth. I couldn't deny him; I sighed against him, content. It was a while before we resurfaced; too much had happened. I missed him so much! The kiss became desperate as I attempted to memorize his touch . . . his taste again. I breathed him in, holding on to him for balance in the sea of emotions roiling within me. He pulled back suddenly, staring down at me, his eyes smoldering with desire.

"I guess I needed that," I said. "I was babbling. I never babble. I am always so in control—maybe that's part of the problem, I feel like I have been so out of control since I met you—"

Nicolas kissed me again, sliding his hand beneath the familiar blue-patterned gown to run along my hip to my thigh. I was completely bare, the nurses having removed everything during the examinations. Nicolas pulled back suddenly, and I could feel his response to the new knowledge against my thigh. He shifted in an attempt to relieve his discomfort. I couldn't help chuckling deviously with awareness of his response. "I did it again, didn't I, but the results are quite worth it."

"Minx," he replied, brushing his lips against the corner of my mouth. "I think it is great that you found your father. I would love to meet him, Ieshelle."

"I have a half brother too. His name is Benjamin; he lives in Britain. I haven't met him yet. He was due to come back to the island, but I had to leave to come back and get you."

"Mmmm. So, you were coming back to get me?"

"Yes, I mean, no, I mean, I was—"

He kissed me again, this one quick. "Calm down. Try again."

I took a moment to catch my breath before beginning again.

"I was coming back to see . . . to ask you . . . I wanted to know if you still loved me." I dropped my eyes, unable to meet his. His face had been so absent of emotion when he walked in . . . but he had kissed me. Passion had never been a problem between us, but had I destroyed the love he felt for me?

He brushed his hand across my cheek, lifting my face to his. His eyes were so blue, I was lost in their depths. "I never stopped loving you, Ieshelle. I don't think it's possible."

"But I pushed you away . . . more than once. I didn't believe that I deserved someone like you. You broke down all my walls. I had nowhere to hide!"

"You don't need to hide from me, Ieshelle, not ever. I love you, and I'm sorry I wasn't patient enough but I needed you with me."

"You're sorry? I should be apologizing to you— for not trusting you, trusting in us! I'm sorry for that. I caused us to lose so much time together, and life is too short. My mother and Eden Rose said as much, and Damien proved it."

"Yes, life is too short, Ieshelle, and that's why I want us to get married as soon as you're feeling up to it. That is . . . if you will have me."

I shook my head. "We don't have to get married, Nicolas. I am happy to just . . . I don't want there to be any pretense between us."

Nicolas kissed me again, silencing my rambling once more. "You know nothing, Ieshelle. I want to marry *you*. I have always wanted you. I stated that from the beginning. The fact that you are carrying our baby is not the issue. I want to marry you because I love you. I want you to carry my name. I want to make a home with you. You are the mirror to my heart, my soul." Nicolas kissed me again, this time slowly sealing the declaration.

I trailed my hand along his cheek, caressed his ear, until my hand rested at the nape of his neck. "We're having a baby, Nicolas," I whispered against his lips. "My mother predicted it in a letter she left me. How she knew, I don't know, but she was right. How do you feel about that?"

Sixty

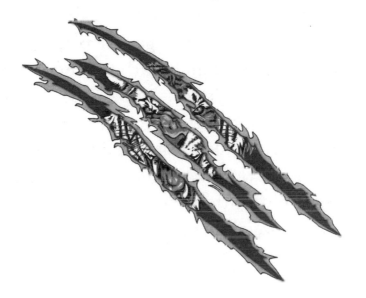

How did I feel about the prospect of becoming a father? Shocked! I had never considered it. I knew I wanted a family someday but hadn't considered when that would be. I was focused on my career. This prospect brought out the fierce, protective instincts within me again. *How could I ensure their safety in my absence? How could I be*

apart from them for an hour, a day, a month? I ran my hand over Ieshelle's still-flat abdomen, the muscles contracting beneath my touch. I couldn't believe it. I was in awe of it all.

"It's fascinating that a part of both of us is growing within you," I said. "There is no greater testament to our love, Ieshelle, than a child."

She seemed to relax against me, as if she had been holding her breath. "Then I accept, Nicolas. I'll marry you."

I held her to me and settled her head against my chest again. Holding my future in my hands—the phrase had never made as much sense as it did in that moment.

We must have dozed off because the nurse came in to shoo me out while she completed her follow-up assessment on Ieshelle to prepare for discharge. Ieshelle was still sleeping, and as I ran my hand over her cheek, she turned into me, her eyes fluttering open. I nodded toward the nurse, who was waiting patiently.

"I need to fill out some paperwork so that we can go home," I told her.

Ieshelle nodded her head in understanding. I kissed her quickly on the lips before exiting the room. Dr. Bartholomew stood outside, and I stepped up to her anxious to hear the news.

She smiled at me. "It seems that you are both doing well enough to go home. Ms. Jones will need the bandage to her head changed once a day. She should follow up as soon as possible with her primary care physician. The stitches will need to be removed in a week. If she experiences blurred vision, excruciating headaches, or bleeding from the ears, nose, or mouth, return her to the hospital immediately. I have prescribed pain medication that is safe for her in her condition. She needs to follow up with an obstetrician, but the baby looks good— no signs of distress. Ms. Jones has not had any spotting or contractions. If she should have any vaginal bleeding or cramping, be sure to bring her back to the hospital immediately. I am also going to give her a script for prenatal vitamins and iron pills because her levels are a little low. She needs to eat sensible meals, drink plenty of fluids, as tolerated, and get plenty of rest. You can resume sexual relations once she has been cleared by her OB doctor."

Changing bandages, bleeding from ears, nose, and mouth? Vaginal bleeding? I tried not

to panic as I took mental notes of everything
Dr. Bartholomew was saying. She handed me
the prescriptions, and I signed the paperwork.
When I turned around, a nurse was wheeling
Ieshelle up to me, a thick white hospital blanket
on her shoulders and legs.

"That takes care of Ms. Jones. Now for *your*
discharge."

"What?" I said swinging back around to face
the doctor.

"Your bandage needs to be changed once a
day unless it becomes soiled or wet. You need
to keep mobility to the arm, but no heavy lifting
or strenuous workouts for a week so that the
wound has enough time to heal and will not
reopen. The stitches are absorbable, so they
won't need to be removed. I have prescribed
you some pain medication in case you need it.
Drink plenty of fluids, and eat sensible meals
each day."

She handed me my discharge papers to sign
and then rushed off as her pager sounded again.
I turned back to Ieshelle, who was smiling, but
I noted the signs of fatigue around her eyes. It
was time to get her home. Frank and the guys
had left earlier. I helped Ieshelle into the car

and fastened her seat belt, noting her eyes were already closing as she reclined in the seat. I kissed her cheek before walking around the car to slide into the driver's seat. I took Ieshelle's hand in mine, needing to touch her, if only through the small caress. When we pulled up into the driveway of her house, Ieshelle sat up with a start.

"I thought we were going home, Nicolas," she said tentatively.

"We are home, *mon ange*."

"But I thought—"

"Ieshelle, my house was just that—a house. This house is a home—our home," I declared as I leaned over to seal the avowal with a kiss. We were home.

Sixty-One

OCHO RIOS, JAMAICA
EIGHT WEEKS LATER . . .

I looked out from my bedroom window over the sprawling lands of my father's estate. I glanced back to the large four- poster bed, longing to get back in. The scar on my forehead was healed and no longer looked red and puffy. The cosmetic surgeon I had consulted thought it would heal nicely. I took note of the bottles of pills that now lined the nightstand and smiled faintly. There was an iron supplement because my iron level was still low, folic acid to help the baby's development and prevent birth defects, and then there were the prenatal vitamins that made my stomach roll and made me gag with the smell. The baby was doing fine and letting his presence be known, as morning sickness and sometimes day sickness was my new enemy.

I missed Nicolas. He had insisted on sleeping in separate beds when we returned from the hospital, going on and on about potential vaginal bleeding, and a potential concussion. I guess he was really shaken up with everything that happened. He didn't want anything to happen to me or the baby. The obstetrician had cleared me a week ago, but Nicolas figured if we had abstained this long, we could wait until our wedding night. He kept going on about how we had done everything out of order and we could try to do it right. He said we needed to practice patience, whatever that meant. Nicolas made sure that we went out on a date at least once a week when he was not on location for the movie. He said he had a lot to make up for, and I enjoyed the time together. I walked into the bathroom, hoping that I could brush my teeth fast enough before the smell of the toothpaste made me hurl. It was a race that I had been losing for the past couple of days. There were still some things I needed to settle before the guests started arriving tomorrow. Nicolette had been a dream, helping in every way, and because she had orchestrated so many of these events, I let her have free rein. I had been so tired lately that it was easy to let her take over while I just played overseer.

I hadn't realized how affluent my father was or that so many dignitaries and high-profile citizens of the island would be attending the wedding. Eden Rose, Jacob, Brian, and Alexis would be here, as well as the entire bike club of DIVAS and an abundance of my staff from both offices. I had not expected so many of them to come, but I was grateful for their love and support. I hadn't realized how much they cared about me. It only reinforced to me that I was not alone, as I had once thought. Nicolas's parents were due to arrive the next morning, as well as some of his family and friends. I couldn't believe that we were getting married in three days. *Three days!*

I looked to the stack of paperwork I had to review before Michelle, the new director of the Las Vegas office, was due to arrive. Once I sat down with Nicolas and really talked about what we could do, it all seemed to fall into place. I hired a director for the Houston office and soon-to-be San Antonio office, as Consetta had resumed her duties in the Dallas office. Nicolas and I decided that our home base would be Las Vegas, and we would live between there and New Mexico when he was training. I was even looking into opening an office in Albuquerque.

Nicolas had to leave shortly after I was discharged from the hospital to start shooting the movie and had returned a week ago, as his character was not due to return until several scenes later in the movie. He was back for two weeks—just long enough for us to get married and enjoy a brief honeymoon on the island.

The time apart had been the worst, but I spent most of the time resting and re-organizing the offices. The time flew by, and Nicolas bought me a new tablet so that we could Facetime each other whenever we wanted. It was great. I could actually see him and talk to him. According to Nicolas, the movie was going great, and he had already received an offer for another movie after this one was completed. He would be playing another supporting role, but there was a bigger part in it for him. Everything was coming together.

I stepped out into the hall. The skirt of the white spaghetti- strapped sundress I was wearing floated around my ankles in soft ruffles. The dress was light and airy and fit snuggly around my growing bust. I wore silver thong sandals, and my hair, still curly from the shower, was pulled back from my face with a white elastic headband, the ebony locks now falling well below my shoulder blades. Silver bangles and earrings were my only jewelry, besides the 4 ½ carat princess-cut diamond in a platinum setting that adorned my left hand. I looked down at the ring that Nicolas had presented to me the morning after we left the hospital following the fight. It was beautiful! Engraved on the band were the words, *"You are never alone, for I am always with you. Nicolas."* I wiped at my eyes, not believing that I was crying yet again. My emotions had been uncontrollable lately; my hormones were all over the place.

The estate was truly magnificent, and my father had given us a brief overview of the history when we arrived. The house was one of the oldest on the island, and the gardens were renowned for their beauty and exquisite flowers. I spent most of the afternoons in the gardens, relaxing. My father had a green thumb—his roses were some of the most beautiful that I had ever seen. He also had an abundance of local flora growing, along with a vegetable garden, the produce of which Annabel and Josie, my father's loyal servants, used in the kitchen for the meals.

I wouldn't have believed that I would grow to care about my father so much so soon, but I did. Barnabus was generous, and his heart was genuine. I could see why my mother loved this gentle, caring, compassionate, and giving man. I headed downstairs in search of breakfast, as my stomach finally had settled and was ready to receive some form of nourishment. Nicolette was probably already there, pestering Anna and Josie for recipes.

As I approached the kitchen, I was alarmed to hear what sounded like a shouting match. Curious as to who could be causing such a ruckus, I pushed through the swinging door.

Sixty-Two

"Just who are you? You couldn't possibly be the one claiming to be my father's long-lost daughter. And where is Anna? I need my coffee," a man demanded.

"What are you blathering on about? I know Barnabus raised you better. Where are your manners?" Nicolette sounded like a schoolmarm. I started to speak up, but she took the lead. They were both completely oblivious to my presence.

"Usually people start the morning using common sense and good manners, something I will chalk up to jet lag for you today. Good morning, Benjamin, as you could be no other. No, I am not Barnabus's long-lost daughter, but my sister-in-law is. I am Nicolette St. Pierre. As for Miss Anna, she is down in the gardens with Miss Josie and Barnabus, collecting fresh vegetables for lunch and dinner today. If you are in search of coffee, there is a fresh pot on the stove. You can help yourself. As far as breakfast, that was finished over two hours ago. However," she added sweetly, "I would be happy to whip up a late brunch, but only if you ask me nicely."

Nicolette was dressed in a flowing mandarin-colored sheath that stopped mid-thigh and highlighted the gold in her hair while defining the blue in her eyes. Her hands rested on her hips in exasperation.

"I will do no such thing!" he responded indignantly.

"Fine. Your loss," Nicolette responded nonchalantly before returning to peruse the newspaper.

"Where is your sister-in-law now?" Benjamin asked, his voice seeming stern.

"Your *sister*, Ieshelle. That is her name. I-E-S-H-E-L-L-E. She is upstairs resting, if you must know."

"It has yet to be proven that she is my sister," Benjamin countered.

I tried not to take offense and looked at it from his point of view. It was quite mind-boggling that only after my mother passed I would find a letter that led me to my father. I had to think that some people in the world probably would take advantage of such a situation, but Benjamin was out of line. After I spoke with him initially on the phone, he had been elusive. I hadn't actually spoken to him since that first time; we'd communicated only through messages via voicemail. I had been excited about meeting him. Other than my father, Benjamin was the only family I had in this world, and I needed my family now, especially with the baby.

"There are no tests or documentation to prove this claim," Benjamin insisted.

"Only because your father refused," Nicolette countered. "He doesn't need any 'proof' to know that Ieshelle is his daughter." Benjamin looked shocked to learn that our father had refused blood tests.

"No matter. I will form my own opinions," he said.

"Seems to me you have already," Nicolette said. "In fact, I would say that you seem to have this whole thing worked out. Sad to think that you are so wrong. Being a royal pain in the ass this weekend will not only hurt your sister but your father as well."

"I know nothing about this woman. For all I know, she could be a con artist and you and your brother her accomplices," Benjamin snarled.

"You're a bastard! Ieshelle is no con artist. She is one of the nicest people I know, and I am happy to have her as a part of my family. If you took the time to get to know her, you would see that. She is a successful businesswoman who owns her own company with offices in Las Vegas, Dallas, Houston, and soon, San Antonio, and Albuquerque."

I stepped fully into the room before she could say more. "Nicolette, it's okay," I said. "I can understand where Benjamin is coming from. Everything has happened so fast. I had hoped . . . no matter. Maybe it wasn't a good idea to have the wedding here. I'll talk to my father."

With that said, I turned and fled the room as tears blurred my vision. I couldn't understand why I was crying. I understood Benjamin's point of view, but that didn't stop the pain I felt at his rejection. As I hurried toward the garden, I didn't see Nicolas until I ran smack into him.

"*Mon ange*, what has happened? Why are you crying?"

I shook my head, unable to speak as I pushed past him into the garden.

◆ ◆ ◆

What the hell was going on? I moved to follow Ieshelle but heard Nicolette's voice raised in alarm. I saw Barnabus consoling Ieshelle, so I headed to the kitchen to see what was going on with Nicolette—and stepped into a war zone.

"You pompous bastard! Now you've done it. How do you think your father is going to take it that his own son doesn't trust his judgment? You really are an idiot. And to think your father spoke so highly of you!"

Benjamin looked stunned but then recovered. "I didn't know she was standing there."

"It doesn't matter. You're still a selfish bastard."

"Well, you're a brat!"

"Wow, really? Is that the best you can come up with? I was expecting more of an Oxford graduate!"

"Well, at least I did graduate, which is more than I could say for the likes of you. What do you do? Model?"

"You chauvinistic son of a bitch!" Nicolette reached back and landed a solid blow to his right cheek, the force strong enough to snap his head back. *Good girl*, I thought. *She remembered to close her fist and wrap her thumb around on the outside.* I stood back to watch the reaction, knowing that if he laid one hand on her, I would end him, Ieshelle's brother or not. He had been the reason why Ieshelle was crying, and now I saw why.

"Why, you little bitch!" He stepped up then and grabbed her to him. That was it. He had made Ieshelle cry and now he was manhandling Nicolette. I had had enough.

"Get your hands off her, now!"

"And just who are you? No, let me guess. You must be her boyfriend. I would expect someone who looks like her to be dating a tool like you."

"You really are a pompous bastard!" I said, just before I gave him a stealth blow against the same jaw, pulling it at the end, for some reason not wanting to break the bone. The impact snapped his head backward, causing him to release Nicolette and fall back on his ass. The small satisfaction I felt at the act did not dissipate my anger. I stood over him as he attempted to gain his bearings. The blow must have caused his head to spin because he looked dazed. "My name is Nicolas St. Pierre, Nicolette is my sister, and Ieshelle is my wife-to-be and the mother of my son. If I ever see you touch my sister again, I will give you a repeat, but if you ever make my woman cry again, I will end you! You got it?"

Benjamin looked stunned, as he held his hand to his jaw checking to see if it was broken. I knew it wasn't. Deep down, I knew that in spite of the insults that Ieshelle would not be happy if I broke her brother's jaw. He still hadn't answered, so I stepped closer until he put his hands up in surrender. "I've got it completely."

I nodded my acceptance of his acknowledgment, just as Nicolette stepped up to him, shaking her head. "That's strike two, Oxford boy! Strike three, and you're out!"

◆ ◆ ◆

Will Nicolette discover a love of her own? Will Ieshelle and Nicolas say I do, or will Benjamin cause a scandal that will threaten everything?

See the conclusion of this story in the upcoming sequel, *Recipe for Love.*